Advance praise for

KNOW THE MOTHER

"The stories in *Know the Mother* are like jewels—glittering, finely wrought, and worthy of careful appraisal. Here is fiction that examines not only the everyday messiness of living but the painful miracle of birth and the beautiful mystery of death with equal insight. Cooper's elegant, wise, and energetic collection is about what it means to be a woman, a mother, a sister, a wife, a child, and most of all, human."

—Angela Flournoy, author of *The Turner House*

"Each one of these short, short stories is as full of excitement, triumphs, and losses as a movie or novel but as easy to swallow and as satisfying as bonbons. A perfect bedtime accompaniment, *Know the Mother* is a great gift for friends. Cooper shines a brilliant light on the everyday, on the little things as real, and as unexpected, as the opening of our hearts."

—Toi Derricotte, author of *The Undertaker's Daughter* and recipient of a Guggenheim and two National Endowment for the Arts fellowships. She is also a chancellor of the Academy of American poets and the co-founder of Cave Canem, a home for black poetry.

"Desiree Cooper's *Know the Mother* is a collection of thirty vignettes that examine how migrations changed the fabric of families and particularly motherhood. Young women had to make their own way—to forge for themselves the demarcation between home and the outside world, what was expected of them, and what goals they had to live up to. Motherhood was no longer cast in the direct shadow of grandmothers, and mothers-in-law, but rather shaped by the social and cultural biases of racism and sexism through which they navigated, seemingly alone. If motherhood was the icing on the cake, she held together what was under that icing. Should the mother remain unchanged, a fixer or a giver commanded merely by her role?"

—Colleen J. McElroy, author of *Blood Memory*

KNOW
THE
MOTHER

MADE IN MICHIGAN WRITERS SERIES

GENERAL EDITORS
Michael Delp, Interlochen Center for the Arts

M. L. Liebler, Wayne State University

ADVISORY EDITORS
Melba Joyce Boyd, *Wayne State University*

Stuart Dybek, *Western Michigan University*

Kathleen Glynn

Jerry Herron, *Wayne State University*

Laura Kasischke, *University of Michigan*

Thomas Lynch

Frank Rashid, *Marygrove College*

Doug Stanton

Keith Taylor, *University of Michigan*

A complete listing of the books in this series can be found online at wsupress.wayne.edu

KNOW
THE
MOTHER

stories by
DESIREE COOPER

WAYNE STATE UNIVERSITY PRESS

DETROIT

20 19 18 17 16   5 4 3 2 1

Library of Congress Cataloging Number: 2015954823

ISBN 978-0-8143-4149-0 (paperback)
ISBN 978-0-8143-4150-6 (ebook)

Publication of this book was made possible by a generous gift
from The Meijer Foundation. Additional support provided by
Michigan Council for Arts and Cultural Affairs and National
Endowment for the Arts.

Designed and typeset by Bryce Schimanski
Composed in Adobe Caslon Pro

*To Mary, Bettie, and my mother, Barbara—the women
to whom I owe my dreams.*

The source of life is as a mother. Be fond of both mother and children but know the mother dearer, and you outlive death.

Tao Te Ching

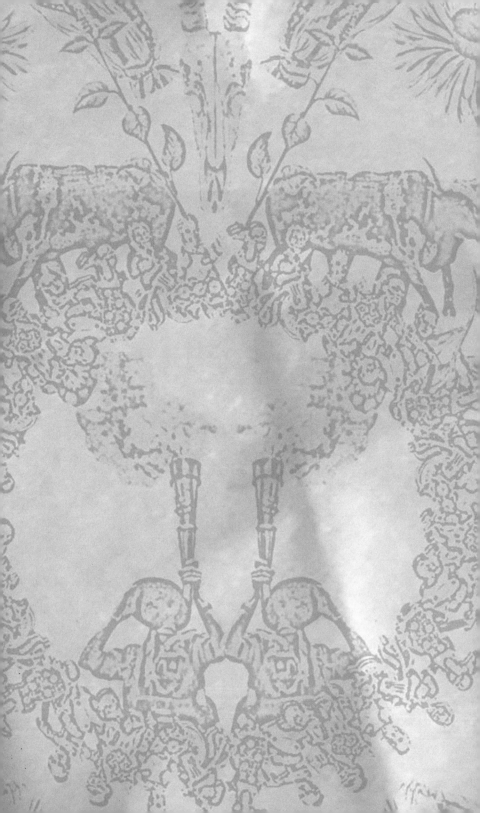

CONTENTS

WITCHING HOUR 1

FEEDING THE LIONS 3

AWAY FROM THE WOODSMAN 5

ICHTHYOPHOBE 9

ONE CANDLE LEFT 13

LAUGHTER AND CAPRICE 19

QUEEN OF THE NILE 23

REPORTING FOR DUTY, 1959 27

KNOW THE MOTHER 37

PRINCESS LILY 39

CARTOON BLUE 41

NIGHT COMING 43

MOURNING CHAIR 55

CEILING 59

ORIGINS OF SACRIFICE 61

IN THE GINZA 65

HOME FOR THE HOLIDAYS 69

73 FIFTEEN ITEMS OR LESS

77 SOFT LANDING

81 SOMETHING FALLS IN THE NIGHT

85 LEFTOVERS

87 ON THE RIM

89 THE DISAPPEARING GIRL

93 GRAVEYARD LOVE

97 NOCTURNE

101 POSTBELLUM LOVE STORY

105 SECOND SLEEP

107 TO THE BONE

111 REQUIEM FOR A DRESS

115 OPEN SKY

119 THE MASSAGE

123 ACKNOWLEDGMENTS

KNOW
THE
MOTHER

WITCHING HOUR

WHY DO WE WAKE EACH NIGHT IN THAT SPIRITLESS moment between worlds, we mothers and daughters and wives? And why does the night abandon us to twinkling worry, to the rattling breaths of our children, to the hard floor of our long prayers? What fresh dangers tap against the black window? And why do our men snore so easily while the horror gathers? Why is it always at three fifteen that evil drags us from beneath the red wine or white pills to make us sit up and see the world so clearly? Who comes to whisper our names and turn our blood to sludge? Where is the mercy for those of us who lie awake, weeping in the eternal hours before the crucifixion?

FEEDING
THE LIONS

MY FEET FLIP-FLOP LOUDLY INTO MY FATHER'S ROOM. In the months that I have been taking care of him, I have become noisy, like a Hmong girl with jangles on her ankles to shoo away the evil spirits. As long as I'm making noise, Pop won't startle when I appear by his side.

Even with his numb feet and useless eyes, Pop likes to rise each morning and dress himself. I lay out clean, matching clothes for him every night, just like my mother used to do. This morning, he has mis-buttoned his green-and-white-striped shirt, but I don't correct him.

"So you're already up, I see."

He lifts his chin proudly in the direction of my voice and smiles. His smile is quavering and gummy, not at all like the swaggering smile in the picture of him on the dresser—combat helmet tilted back, his arm around his army buddy in Da Nang.

"I'm doing your sheets this morning, OK?" I am all business. Tenderness, he has taught me, only erodes courage. "What are you watching?"

I flinch at the word "watching," but he doesn't seem to notice. He points the remote in the direction of the TV. "The Lions drafted

Spivey in the second round. They don't need a goddamn cornerback. What they need is a coach."

I duck when I pass between him and ESPN—a wasted gesture. The air fills with the tinge of sweat, urine, and rot as I yank the sheets from the bed. I want to open a window, but I can't risk the sound of a backfiring engine or a siren sending him into a panic.

His dresser is filled with the prescriptions that I spoon to him like Halloween candy. In the dresser mirror, I can see new wrinkles framing my eyes. I am a cocktail of genes—my mother's hair, black as bean paste, but as unruly and thick as my father's. My teak skin is not like his skin, which is Southern-gravy brown. If it weren't for his cloudy eyes, you'd never guess he had survived both Selma and Saigon.

"At least the Lions got the number-two pick," Pop says to his lap. "That'll buy them one sorry-ass win next year." The morning sun lights the bumpy range along his temples, the remnant scarring of Agent Orange. I can't stand the way, in his blindness, he holds his head down all of the time. It fills me with shame, as if I were seeing him naked.

"Need to put some glue on the quarterback's hands. Can't catch worth shit."

"Toast and eggs coming up," I say. Nursemaid is a much easier role to play than daughter. "How 'bout blueberry jam this morning?"

"Strawberry. I hate blueberry."

I wish he would talk to me, just once, without barking orders. I'm nearly out of the door with the bundle of dirty sheets when I hear him say, "Come sit, Quyen."

Hearing him say my mother's name makes my heart stop. I glance back and his head is up, his murky eyes staring at me, but he is somewhere else.

AWAY FROM
THE WOODSMAN

I JUMP OUT OF THE JEEP ALMOST BEFORE DADDY CAN
park. Lucky bounds after me as the December morning burns my
cheeks.

"Hold your horses!" Mom warns when I take off to run circles in
the snow. Lucky rolls in the fluffy powder beside me, tongue flapping,
his black Lab nose dusted white.

"I get to pick!" I shout happily. It's so good to gulp the searing
air after the stuffy ride, the sweet smell of Mom's "Night Charms"
mixing with Daddy's breath, which is always bitter and mediciney.

Daddy wobbles out of the car and shoulders the ax. Mom has
been quiet the whole ride. She is hiding behind her dark glasses,
which she wears even in the house. She shoves her hands deep into
her pockets as we tromp across the glistening grove. The snow squeaks
beneath my pink, polka-dotted boots. I reach for Daddy's hand—the
one without the ax—and smile up at him. When I touch him, he
blinks out of his thoughts, then smiles back.

Mom is doing her usual—trying her best not to have fun. Four
steps behind, I can hear her say, "Brrrrr!" just like a cartoon character.

5

"C'mon, Mom." I reach for her hand, wishing that she could just be happy like Dad.

"Yeah, Mom," Dad says. "Don't be a spoilsport."

She takes my hand but says nothing. We walk together, a perfect family on Christmas Eve. I sing, "O Tannenbaum, O Tannenbaum," over and over because I don't know the rest of the words.

Ahead in the grove, Lucky is circling a Scotch pine that looks just like a Christmas cookie. "That's the one, Lucky!" I yell, letting go of my parents' hands.

"That one's too big, Missy," Mom says practically. "It won't fit in the cabin."

"Well, now!" Dad announces like a circus ringmaster. "Who died and left you the boss of Christmas? If this is the one my princess wants, this is the one we're gonna get!" His laughter overrides Mom's silent protest. Lucky barks and wags his tail.

"Stand back." Dad takes the Gränsfors Bruk in both hands. It's Farfar's ax, all the way from Sweden. It has spent three lonely years pegged high on a wall in the outdoor shed. Since Farfar died, Dad hardly ever wants to spend Christmas at the cabin.

Swaying slightly as he lifts the ax, Dad swings hard at the base of the tree. The ax bounces a little, barely gnawing into the trunk. He steps back, breathes deeply, and grunts as he takes a second swing. The pine tree shudders at the shock of the first cut.

"Erik, let's go home and talk." Mom tugs gently on Dad's coat, but he shoves her back so hard, she nearly falls on her backside. Mom's mouth opens in an O like a gingerbread girl and she stares at the spot on her chest where Dad pushed her. I reach down and hide my face in Lucky's fur. Why does Mom always have to press it?

Dad yanks hard to dislodge the ax from the wounded trunk. His jaws harden and his mouth clamps tight. He hacks angrily but the tree holds on, barely giving to Dad's ax. He swings and swings again, his face purpling as the tree resists. Each thud shudders across the snow and into my boots. Dad's breath billows like a dragon's.

My head starts to pound in the sharp winter light. I don't want the tree anymore; I wish I could make him stop. Instead, I shrink against Mom, who takes me into her trembling arms. One final swing and there is a snap like broken bone. Mom screams and shelters me as the tree topples toward Daddy. I am astonished; in the movies, the tree always falls away from the woodsman.

For a few seconds, there is nothing but frozen quiet.

Mom lets go of me and I run toward Dad. He is kneeling beside the tree, which is spread-eagle in the snow. It's larger than it had seemed standing against the sky. I can see that it will never fit through our cabin door.

The smell of pine sap makes my stomach lurch, but I stuff down the urge to heave. "You did it, Dad," I say, trying to rescue his mood.

He stands slowly, then ruffles my hair. "Let's get this thing home," he says.

He grabs a branch while I tug at another. We drag it toward the car, leaving a sprinkle of needles behind.

ICHTHYOPHOBE

LESLIE WAS ONLY FOUR WHEN SHE FOUND HER MOTHER doubled in pain on the bathroom tiles. Water trickled down her mother's legs, smelling of a clear, sweet spring.

"Call Daddy, just like we practiced," Mommy panted, her face tightening with a contraction. Leslie had never seen her mother so animal. She pressed the speed dial on the phone, the way Daddy had shown her only two weeks earlier.

"Mommy's in the bathroom hurting," Leslie reported.

That's a good girl. You stay with Mommy until I get there.

You're my little champ.

Don't cry—you'll scare Mommy.

You are so brave.

Daddy and the ambulance arrived at the same time. They found Leslie sitting on the bathroom floor, clutching a teddy bear and rubbing her mother's taut, white belly.

That night, Auntie Rose stayed with Leslie. "You are such a big girl—not even one tear!" Auntie Rose stroked Leslie's sandy hair. "Your new baby brother is so proud of you."

In a bowl on the dresser, Leslie's goldfish opened and closed its mouth, glub, glub, glub. She stared without blinking into its flooded gullet, all the way down to its fluttering heart.

ॐ

The boys decide they want to spend the last day of their vacation fishing on Mirror Lake.

"C'mon, Mom!" Jake and Justin chide. "It'll be fun!"

Of course it will be fun, Leslie tells herself as her sons splash from the shore to the drift boat. But she can't seem to shake a feeling of dread as her husband Matt situates the boys on the middle bench.

"OK, here you go." Matt smiles reassuringly as he helps Leslie aboard. She wants to suggest they go hiking instead, but she doesn't want to seem like a wet blanket. Matt gives her waist a squeeze, then abandons her to start the outboard. As she settles in, the boys snap on orange life vests that stink of mildew.

Suddenly, they are slicing through the murky mountain lake. Closing her eyes, Leslie doesn't let herself imagine the life lapping beneath the water. Instead, she sucks in the sharp Montana air and tries to relax.

By the time Matt cuts the motor, the sun has burned away the morning scrim and the sky is infinite blue. Lacy, green mountains shadow the water. As Jake and Justin excitedly bait their lines, Matt kicks back on his end of the boat and tilts his hat forward to snooze. Leslie feels her muscles go lax—maybe this will be a beautiful end to a great vacation, she tells herself.

Nearly two hours pass. The fun is melting in the heat of the aluminum boat. Just as the boys are starting to get hungry and whiny, something from the depths swallows Jake's hook. Leslie's stomach clenches as the line goes taut.

Justin cheers his brother on: "You got one! Pull it in!"

Leslie's heart is a scuttling eel. There is nowhere to run. Matt bolts upright and spreads his legs wide to steady the boat as Jake delivers the fat cutthroat trout with red slashes on its jaw, its belly bulging white. Justin lunges after it with two hands as the thing beats itself against the deck.

Leslie curls into herself. She had vowed she wouldn't do this, but here she is, screaming. She is like the trout, suffocating in the rich mountain air.

Finally, the fish stills, hanging lifeless with a hook through its face. From her end of the boat, Leslie watches as Jake raises his line in triumph, the power over life gleaming in his eyes.

ONE CANDLE LEFT

LITTLE WALTER SAT ALONE AT THE END OF THE LONG table in the noisy Doughboy Pizzeria, where fourteen kids from his third-grade class had come for his birthday. They were scattered all around the pizzeria, playing video games or shooting basketballs or enjoying the violent hilarity of Whac-a-Mole. Having been coerced to attend the party by their polite mothers, none of them had bothered to sit at the table with the birthday boy for long. None except the allergy-infested Sammy Patel, who perched uncomfortably in a chair at the other end of the table.

"Don't you two want to go play?" asked Sarah, Walter's mother, hovering over her son like a thought balloon.

He was an only child, even though Sarah had always dreamed of a magical horde of children, like the Von Trapps. But in the doctor-filled years since Walter's birth, it had become evident that there would be no more babies. So she'd dangled poor Walter into the world like a sticky fly strip. Maybe her freckled son would draw other people's children into her life. At least then her dreams of den mothering and sleepovers and backyard campouts would be fulfilled.

But Walter didn't make friends easily. He was stoic and simple, like his dad. Blue veins rivered dangerously close to the surface of his ghostly skin. His dark eyes were set so close, he had the beady stare of a crow. His limbs were scrawny and ill-suited. He seemed to attract only kids with old souls, poor eyesight, and premature potbellies. Kids like Sammy Patel.

"Leave him alone, for God's sake, Sarah. It's his birthday." Hank put down the camera—there was nothing to photograph but the empty table and the Spider-Man paper plates—and gave Walter's shoulders a coach-like slap. "You're having a great time, aren't you, son?"

Walter nodded obligingly. He immediately noticed a downward twitch of his mother's smile and a tightening of his father's grip on his shoulders. He realized that somehow, he had just chosen sides.

"Pizzas for Walter Shea?" asked an acne-faced teen in a khaki uniform.

Sweaty, bickering kids appeared from nowhere, like alchemy. "Pizza! Pizza!"

Sarah's mood lightened. The last few weeks had taken a toll: the preparation for the party; the incessant calls to the parents to make sure that they showed up with their beautiful, cruel children; the trip down the aisles at Toys "R" Us, wondering what would please a nine-year-old boy who was bad at everything. Her stomach was a jittery tangle; it had been a week since she'd been able to keep anything down. Even today, with everything going so well, she felt faint.

"Everyone take a seat!" she directed, not letting the nausea ruin her perfect party. "Hank, put the cheese pizza down on that end— Khalid, Ben, and Ruthie, stay away from the pepperoni. Sammy, here's your personal pizza, no cheese." The lactose-intolerant Sammy smiled gratefully. "OK, everyone, eat up!" Sarah clapped.

Hank resisted rolling his eyes. His darling wife loved staging events where she could bark orders and create spectacular special effects. She wasn't a mother—she was a producer. Even when they were home alone, everything was a little too bright, a little too worthy of an audience.

It hadn't always been that way. Sarah's showmanship blossomed after the fertility specialist pinpointed Hank as the problem. Since then, it seemed that every itemized shopping trip, every carefully orchestrated vacation, every meticulously planned dinner party was Sarah's way of glossing over her disappointment. Disappointment in Hank. Disappointment in the fragile Walter.

Why couldn't she just relax and be grateful for all that they had? Why couldn't she be more like Sammy's mom, the widow Vanita Patel, with her elegant silks and positive immigrant outlook? Unlike Sarah, who believed that the worst was always about to befall Walter, Mrs. Patel exuded a blind faith in her plump, stuffy-nosed Sammy. "He's going to be a doctor," she'd once bragged at a PTA meeting. "He is excellent at maths." Hank was intoxicated by her English accent; the delicate, gold ring in her nose; the smell of sandalwood.

Sometimes, when lying in bed next to Sarah, who slept beneath an aromatherapy eye mask, Hank wondered what it would be like to be married to Mrs. Patel and have Sammy—who was at least competing in the Academic Games—as a son. Just thinking about Mrs. Patel made his groin stir, so he cast a guilty glance at Walter, a kid who managed to make mischievous freckles and unruly cowlicks look sad. Maybe it was Hank's fault that his son wasn't something more interesting—like a promising first baseman or a chess champion. He wasn't even somebody's big brother.

It took no time for the kids to plow through the pizza. "Hank, where are the matches?" Sarah whispered conspiratorially, as if every kid hadn't already suspected that the afternoon would involve a blazing cake.

The cake was a relief of Spider-Man, a webbed mound of blue-and-red icing. The nine candles plunged into the superhero's hands, chest, and legs smacked of voodoo. Hank lit them, then stepped back so that Sarah could present the confection to great applause. The children oohed and burst into song.

Through the shimmer of the candlelight, Walter peered at his parents, who had locked arms expectantly. They were posed exactly as they were in the picture on the piano in their living room. The thin smiles on their faces almost looked like love.

Sarah clapped her hands. "C'mon, Walter! Make a wish!"

Hank nodded and added, "Make it good, son!"

Walter gazed from his mother's queasy face to his father's distant expression. The air between parents and child rippled like a mirage. The noise of the pizzeria tamped down. The grease-streaked faces of the children blurred. The room started to spin, and Walter closed his eyes.

All I wish, he thought, wheezing in a mouthful of air, *is for my parents to be happy.*

As Walter sputtered over the cake, a sea roiled in Sarah's stomach. She dashed for the bathroom and fell on her knees in the stall. She had not eaten at all—saving her calories for a slice of birthday cake—but she still wretched over the bowl, bringing up clear bile. She remained in the stall for a long time, her skin dewy, her feet and hands gone cold.

She staggered to the sink and splashed water on her face. In the mirror she looked sunken and pink. *Could I be?* she wondered. She stood there for a long time, weeping in disbelief.

Just as Walter had blown out the candles, Hank noticed how the air felt suddenly humid, like an orchid hothouse. Within seconds, Mrs. Patel appeared, her thin body swathed in red and gold. "I'm just in time!" she laughed, giving Sammy a kiss, then mussing Walter's hair. "How's the birthday boy? Where's Sarah?" she asked Hank, who just grinned, tongue-tied.

"Let me help you with this," she said, her hand lingering tenderly on his before taking away the cake knife.

Hank picked up his camera. Through the lens, he watched Mrs. Patel laughing, her sari slung casually over her shoulder, her easy manner transforming the gathering into a party.

"Smile and say hello!" he said, clicking the shutter just as she turned her astonished gaze directly into the lens.

LAUGHTER
AND CAPRICE

"WHEN IS IT PROPER TO SPIT IN A MAN'S FACE?" CAPRICE asked her first-grade class.

As a student teacher, this was her first day handling the classroom alone. She knew it was risky to begin the morning with a joke—one about spitting, no less. But what better way to endear herself to the children than by evoking the forbidden?

"I know! I know!" Emma Lee Peterson raised her hand and jumped up and down. Her enthusiasm was contagious. In seconds, the whole class was jockeying for attention.

"Calm down! Let's hear Emma Lee's answer first," Caprice said, suddenly nervous. How was she going to corral the beehive of energy that her joke had stirred?

But the children—who were still under the thumb of their regular teacher, the no-nonsense Mrs. Gregory—miraculously quieted. "OK, that's better," Caprice said, relieved. "Now Emma Lee, when is it proper to spit in a man's face?"

Brushing back her thin raven bangs, the eager-to-please Emma Lee lifted her chin and said, "When he keeps beating up everybody in the house and you're sick of it!"

There was a collective hiccup; the class really *wanted* to laugh, but the punch line had nothing to do with boogers or gross food or kooky animals.

Three seconds sat between the new teacher and her students. Three seconds during which Caprice held an expression of delighted surprise while she coiled back into her own childhood. Back to when she, too, was a lanky seven-year-old, running home after school, wearing new pink tennis shoes with soles that lit up every time her feet pounded the sidewalk. Even though it was October in Michigan, she had abandoned her jacket on the playground to run home and show her mother her paper. The one with the bright gold star.

The lights in her shoes went dead as she hesitated on the front steps of the family bungalow. A muddy, blue Ford pick-up was in the driveway. That meant Mike was over.

"Hey, babe!" came her mother's voice from the screen door. "Whatchu got there?"

Caprice's heart warmed whenever her mother smiled, which was seldom. "Look!" Caprice said, offering the paper to her mother as a gift. "I got a gold star!"

The gift should have made her mother happy, but instead, fat tears erupted. "Oh, babe," her mother wept. "You're such a smart girl. So much smarter than me. I'll bet you're gonna be a teacher someday."

Suddenly, Mike was on the porch yanking the paper from her mother's hands. "I was talkin' to you," he said.

"Stay here." Caprice's mother kissed her on the cheek. "I'll be right back."

The door slammed. There was arguing and the sound of things breaking, while Caprice shivered on the front steps. She was afraid to go inside, and more afraid to run away and leave her mother in there alone. So she sat and counted to one hundred by tens, over and over.

Three seconds, and Caprice was back in the classroom with twenty children waiting for her to say something about Emma Lee's joke. But she felt as helpless now as she had as a little girl quaking on the front steps.

"Nope," she said, turning to the chalkboard, unable to face the trembling Emma Lee. "You can only spit in a man's face when his mustache is on fire."

Behind her back, Caprice could hear the riotous sound of children's laughter.

QUEEN OF
THE NILE

THEY WERE DRINKING AT THEIR USUAL TABLE AT THE
rathskeller when someone asked C. Amelia King what the C in her
name stood for.

Frankly, her first name was none of their business, she thought.
Who ever asked that of F. Scott Fitzgerald or D. H. Lawrence? Rim-
ming her whiskey glass with a manicured finger, Amelia winked.

A single, East Coast transplant to Chicago, Amelia carefully
shielded her personal life from her business partners. She kept no
pictures of her family on her desk. Her flirtations always walked
the edge of good taste—a hint of lace, the scent of musk, stilettos
and a glimpse of thigh. Six years into her career and her assets had
landed her senior account executive with a Chicago ad agency. She'd
learned that mystery was nearly as useful as her Stanford degrees.

Especially the mystery of her race. Whenever coworkers tried
to categorize her, she pushed back on their assumptions to keep
them off balance. At dinner at the Caucus Club, a client had once
blushed with embarrassment after he ordered hummus, believing
her to be Arab. Another time, a client just started speaking Span-
ish to her after a meeting. She replied in Japanese. Most often,

people seemed content to err on the side of dusky whiteness—maybe Greek or Italian—allowing her to navigate firm politics more easily.

"Cynthia?" ventured Nate Drummond, who was even more boring than he was cautious. Amelia had often caught Nate gazing at her a bit too long, his pupils dilated like the mouth of a well. Was it her dark hint of Gypsy that made his imagination run wild?

Instead of scoffing at Nate's guess, Amelia laughed good-naturedly, always careful not to show an edge. "Cynthia Amelia," she said, rolling the name in her mouth to try it out. "That sounds awful. My mother hates me, but not that much."

The whole table laughed as Amelia sucked on the Maraschino cherry she'd fished out of her Manhattan.

"Chloe!" someone else suggested.

"Nope," she laughed, enjoying the game of Rumplestiltskin. They'd never guess the moniker that had crowned four generations of Maryland women, going back to the first one to buy her own freedom.

Corinthia. For her family, the name was a source of pride. But for the only black child in her kindergarten class, it was already evident to C. Amelia that Corinthia was not a princess name. At the Sidwell Friends School, she corrected her third-grade teacher: "Call me Corey." By the time she earned her joint MBA-JD at Stanford, she was C. Amelia.

"I've got it!" Nate rallied, emboldened by the game. He smiled crookedly and held up his Glencairn for a toast. "To our lovely Cleopatra."

Cleopatra Amelia King. The table erupted. Amelia's ecru complexion reddened. The men around the table wouldn't stop laughing. Amelia glared at Nate. What was so fucking funny?

Collecting herself, she took the joke amiably, but her stomach felt like an anvil. She tried to talk herself out of being too sensitive. These guys were her friends—they'd been drinking buddies at the Rathskeller since they'd finished grad school.

"You mean like the Queen of the Nile?" another piped in, nearly doubled over.

As Nate threw an arm around Amelia, she tensed. "No, dumb ass," he said, bringing his face so close to Amelia's that she closed her eyes. "Like Cleopatra Jones."

REPORTING FOR DUTY, 1959

"THERE GOES MY BABY!" THE DRIFTERS WARBLED FROM the car radio.

"Keep it there! Keep it there!" twelve-year-old Junior yelled from the back seat as his mother searched for a good station on the AM dial.

"Hold your horses, young man!" said his mother, Joyce, turning to give the evil eye to her boys. "And Curtis, get your feet off the back of my seat."

Nine-year-old Curtis scowled and put his feet on the floor. "When are we going to stop? My legs are going to sleep."

"There goes my baby," crooned the radio. Junior sang along, throwing kisses at his little brother.

"Stop it, booger face!" Curtis yelled, lunging for Junior's throat.

Junior laughed and made huge choking sounds, exaggerating the danger for the benefit of his parents in the front seat.

"Quit it!" yelled Joyce, reaching back to slap whomever was closest.

"He won't stop it!" Curtis protested, clawing desperately at his older brother.

"Help! He's killing me!" wailed Junior.

Sgt. Douglas Carter—who had been calmly chauffeuring his family from the air-force base in San Antonio, Texas, to their new assignment in Tampa, Florida—lifted his foot from the gas pedal. At the same time, he turned off the radio, bringing a pall of silence upon the passengers in the car.

The car slowed. Joyce turned around and looked straight ahead, as if to say, "I tried to save you boys."

Curtis tried not to think about what their father was about to do to them. Instead, he looked intensely out the window, noticing with terror that the oil wells were now moving so slowly past them that he could count them pumping—up, down, up, down—as many as four times before they disappeared out of sight.

The green-on-green 1957 Buick Century came to a complete stop on the shoulder. Junior held his breath. Curtis, suddenly appreciative of his older brother's brawn, slid next to him for protection.

"Daddy," whimpered Curtis, "we'll be good."

Douglas said nothing as he opened the car door and got out. He was magnificent in his air-force blues. Joyce had pressed the creases in his pants with extra-heavy starch so that, despite the fact that they had already spent ten hours in the car traveling from San Antonio to Houston to Pensacola, they'd maintained their cardboard crease.

Douglas coupled his hands over his head and stretched. To Curtis, he looked like a Titan, like the ones in his mythology book, with dark brown arms long enough to touch the sun.

Joyce opened her pocketbook and got out her mother-of-pearl compact. "You boys have done it now," she said as she dabbed the light caramel powder on her nose. "How are we gonna ever get to Tampa if you keep acting like heathens back there?"

Douglas walked slowly around the hood, past the gleaming silver airplane ornament, to the passenger side of the car. The boys sat boxed in by the freeway on one side and their approaching father on the

28

other. He bent to look into their window, his expression stony. They could see their own eyes—round as trapped animals—reflected in his sunglasses. He knocked on the car window to signal them to roll the glass all the way down.

Junior inched over to crank the handle. The window squeaked as it disappeared into the door.

"Yes, sir?" asked Junior meekly.

Douglas took this moment to remove and clean his sunglasses. The boys waited quietly for what seemed like an eternity. "What's going on back here?" he finally asked.

"Nothin', sir, we were just playin'!" said Curtis, jumping to the defense of his big brother.

"Is there a reason you can't seem to listen to your mother when she talks to you?"

"No, sir!" the boys said in unison, like recruits at basic training.

"Is there a reason we need to put our feet all over the seat and fight like we have no home training?"

"No, sir!"

"Good. If I have to stop the car again, it will be lights out for the both of you."

"Yes, sir!"

"Junior, I want you to be my navigator," said Douglas, pulling a AAA map from his shirt pocket. "I want to stay on I-10 East."

Junior reached for the map, understanding that it was being handed to him in lieu of a beating. There would be no second chance.

"Buddy Boy?" said Douglas as he stood up.

"Yes, sir?" asked Curtis, fearing that the spanking had been reserved for him.

"I need a copilot."

Curtis grinned at his brother. "Copilot" sounded like a rank above "navigator."

"You will tell me at any given time if I'm going north, east, south, or west, like I taught you. Remember to look and see where the sun is first."

"Yes, sir!" Curtis said, saluting. He smirked at his brother when his dad saluted him back.

Douglas put his glasses back on and walked slowly around the car to the driver's side. He slid behind the wheel, groaning slightly as he positioned his back against the hot, green vinyl. Starting the car, he eased back onto the highway.

The boys sat quietly, Junior staring intently at the map, Curtis squinting at the sun.

"Dad?" asked Curtis, now able to see only bright, orange-yellow blotches in front of his eyes.

"Yes, son?" said Douglas, diverting his eyes from the road to the rearview mirror long enough to see his youngest blinking in the back seat.

"What's Mom's job gonna be?"

Without hesitating, Douglas cast a smile at his bride of thirteen years.

"She's the communications officer," he said, winking at Joyce.

With that, Joyce turned on the radio and left it where her favorite, Johnny Mathis, was crooning "Misty."

"Daddy, please, let's stay at the Holiday Inn!" begged Junior, noticing the road signs advertising gas, food, and lodging at the next exit.

"We'll see, son, we'll see," Douglas said wearily.

"Doug, the kids are tired and you've put in twelve hours today. Let's try to find a place for the night," said Joyce, reaching back to pull a blanket over Curtis, who'd been asleep since Mobile, Alabama.

Douglas cast a sidelong glance at Joyce. "OK, honey, I'll try the next exit."

"Grrreat!" whooped Junior, imitating Tony the Tiger. He'd seen commercials about the Holiday Inn, with the big color TVs in the rooms and indoor swimming pools. Maybe Mom would let him get into the water after dinner.

They drove in silence for a while. When the exit came up, Douglas hesitated for a moment, but when Joyce sighed heavily, he relented and steered the car to the off-ramp and pulled up to the first gas station.

"I'll just get some gas before we stop for the night," said Douglas, opening the car door and getting out.

Junior shook his little brother awake.

"Curtis! We're going to stay at the Holiday Inn. Wake up!"

"Junior, pipe down," said Joyce. "We're not sure yet what we're going to do."

Junior flung himself back on the seat as if he'd been shot dead. Curtis, waking just in time to see his brother's theatrics, farted.

"Ew! Mom, did you hear that? Curtis farted again!"

Curtis stifled giggles, as Joyce stared out the window. "Here comes your dad," she said ominously.

The boys straightened up in their seats. At the car next to them, a white gas-station attendant pumped gas, while another squeegeed the dried bugs off of a customer's windshield. Douglas walked past them, touching the brim of his air-force cap politely.

"How do?" one attendant mumbled in response. The other kept pumping gas, his back turned on the black man in uniform.

Douglas came back to the car and began pumping his own gas.

Curtis got on his knees and pressed his head against the window, watching his dad stick the nozzle into the gas tank. The yeasty smell of gas filled the car. All the other dads were sitting in their cars,

31

waiting for the gas-station people to serve them. His was the only dad who knew how to pump the gas himself.

Douglas replaced the nozzle and got back into the car.

"OK," he said. "Let's try the Holiday Inn."

The boys wrestled each other in glee. As they neared the hotel, Junior looked up in time to notice the neon sign flashing in the lobby window.

"Dad! It says, 'Vacancy'! They have room for us! Hooray!" cheered Junior. He could feel the cool water of the pool already.

"You never know, son," said Douglas. "Sometimes they forget to turn off the sign when the hotel is full."

Before heading into the lobby, Douglas put on his hat, buttoned his uniform jacket, and took a deep breath. In the back seat, the boys strained their necks like goslings to keep sight of their dad. They watched as he held the door open for a lady and her toddler, then as he strode up to the check-in desk.

A plump white woman with her hair caught up in a netted beehive took one look at him, then fled to the corner. She talked excitedly to a man who wore a black uniform with gold buttons and a brass name tag.

"He couldn't be a real sergeant with that rinky-dink uniform on," Junior informed Curtis.

They watched as the man came around the desk to talk to Douglas, gently touching their father's elbow as he spoke, obviously urging him to move to the side, out of the middle of the lobby.

But Douglas wouldn't move, and when the boys saw their father plant his feet and lean too close to the hotel manager's beet-red face, they reached for each other as if bracing for a storm.

"What's he saying, Mom?" asked Junior.

Joyce had been watching, too, her hand holding the door handle so tightly that blue veins popped up like Highway 10 on Junior's road map. She bit her lip nervously and turned to the boys.

"You guys sit up in your seats and stop climbing on one another," she said, her words dripping fear rather than firmness. "And stop staring at people out of that window. Your dad's just trying to find out if a room is available."

"But it says right there, 'Vacancy,' big as day!" protested Junior.

"That's enough, young man," barked Joyce. "Just sit down and be quiet!"

Junior looked at his mother as if he'd been slapped. The rules were bending, twisting around him—signs not meaning what they said, his mother meeting his questions with anger rather than answers. His father was now pacing in the lobby of the hotel, saying words he could not hear, pointing to the stripes on his uniform, then to his family in the car, while the white man in the rinky-dink uniform kept shaking his head, "No."

It was suddenly all too clear to Junior that there would be no color TV tonight, no clean scent of chlorine as he dove into the deep end of the pool, no thrill of chocolates on his pillow even though he had already brushed his teeth. It wasn't fair.

He reached for the door handle and let himself out.

"Junior!" Joyce called. "Junior, get back into the car this minute! Oh my God! Curtis, you stay right here—" She dashed out of the car behind Junior, leaving Curtis sitting in the back seat bewildered and alone.

Curtis scooted over to Junior's side of the car, the side where his brother had been keeping watch over his dad. He was young enough to be completely immobilized by his mother's command, but old enough to sense the danger of sitting still and doing nothing. He rolled down the window and leaned out as far as he could. He saw his mother collar Junior at the hotel entrance, drag him away from the door, and wrap him in a powerful hug.

"Let me go! Let me go!" screamed Junior.

Curtis tried to keep an eye on his father—for Junior's sake, for his own sake—but he couldn't see well, now that the tears were flowing. He wiped his eyes and a stream of snot from his nose. In that instant, he saw his dad glance outside, to where Joyce and Junior were struggling on the sidewalk.

"Junior, Dad's coming, Dad's coming!" yelled Curtis, knowing that the situation would now be fixed. His dad was on the way.

At the sight of Douglas coming out of the glass doors, Joyce released her son and the boy went flying into his father's arms. The hotel manager was now speaking to a sea of pink faces that had gathered to watch in the lobby.

Curtis saw the cold stares, the unkindness in their eyes. He needed to feel his dad's arms around him, strong and unwavering, to hear his voice say, "It's OK, Buddy Boy, it's OK."

In a panic, he pushed open the door, plunking onto the sidewalk. Not taking the time to tend to his stinging knee, he ran toward the rest of his family screaming, "Daddy! Daddy! Daddy!"

Douglas released Junior at the sound of his little one's cries and knelt on the sidewalk to accept Curtis's desperate hug. He lifted Curtis in his arms and strode toward the car.

"C'mon, everybody, get in," he said, as if it were a foxhole and they were under fire.

They all piled in the front seat, still clinging to each other, the boys crying.

"Let's get out of here, Douglas, before the cops come," said Joyce.

Douglas put the car in gear and sped toward the highway in silence. Curtis sat tightly against his father's side, whimpering. He could feel his dad's heart pounding like pistons beneath the hood. Douglas steered with one hand and held Curtis with the other, trying to shush him.

Junior was sitting bolt upright, panting. Curtis could tell that he was really mad. Mad that he didn't get to sleep in the hotel. Mad that his dad, even though he was an air-force sergeant, hadn't fought hard enough to get them a room.

They were on the highway before anyone said a word.

"Dad, why wouldn't they let us have a room?" asked Junior. The way he said it, with his face stony and his mouth drawn tight, Curtis knew that he wasn't going to accept a typical response like, "You'll understand when you get older," or "Because that's the way it is."

"They did give us a room, son," said Douglas finally. "It was in the back by the staff's closet. The clerk had just told another customer that there were plenty of vacancies, so I asked for a different room closer to the pool. They refused to give it to me, and I refused to take the trash they wanted to give me."

Junior's jaw relaxed, and his fists unfurled. Joyce held a Kleenex over her nose and mouth and wept as she looked out the window. Junior stared at his father, at the steadiness of his father's eyes on the road, the patience of his mouth, the stripes on his sleeve, the eagle insignia on his hat.

KNOW
THE MOTHER

AS I WASH MY MOTHER'S BACK, HER SCENT FILLS MY nostrils. Already, she smells like a garden unearthed, a freshly dug grave. I soak the cloth in warm water and witch hazel; she sighs as I swab her shrunken thighs, her shriveled feet.

"Don't leave me," I plead beneath my breath. She twitches and my heart leaps—maybe she's changed her mind and has decided to stay with me a little longer. But for the next three hours, she gives me nothing to hold on to—not one fluttering eyelid, not a wan smile of possibility. She is leaving me so easily, I wonder if her love ever rose above duty.

Two months ago, I was bringing warm sheets up from the dryer in the basement. As I reached the top of the stairs, I could hear Mother singing. I dashed around the corner, half expecting to see her remaking her bed, lifting the mattress to miter the corners.

But when I reached her room, nothing had changed. Her hair was still a thin layer of down. Her cheeks were still sallow. Her shoulder blades jutted beneath the summer blanket as if she were hiding her favorite book beneath the covers. Yet somehow as she slept, she was a young woman again, singing.

At her bedside, I doze without resting. I dream that my mother is dressed in a black taffeta gown. Her cheeks are rouged with stage makeup, her eyes shimmering. On cue, she makes her way to the curtain. I call her name three times, but nothing I say can make her look back.

PRINCESS LILY

OBJECTS WITH LIKE CHARGES REPULSE EACH OTHER. Objects with opposite charges attract each other. That's what Miss Powers said. She was the physics teacher at Kubasaki High. I was afraid to ask the question that kept rolling around in my head: What happens when a charged object meets a neutral one? Like when Justin cornered me outside of the gym. Like the surprise of his tongue down my throat, choking me with his musky smell in the humid Okinawan spring. Like when I was both repulsed and attracted, a neutral object caught in his electric charge.

Mr. Drake taught geometry. He loved his angles and proofs. By the end of class, his glasses were always dusted with chalk. According to Mr. Drake, two parallel lines can never meet. Never, ever.

But that isn't true. What could be more parallel than the lives of my dad, Col. Nathan Scott, and Mr. Sugimoto, the wiry, ageless man who pedaled his black bicycle to base every Wednesday to give me piano lessons? Their lives intersected when my dad sat down Mr. Sugimoto in the living room and explained to him my "condition." They struggled to communicate because Mr. Sugimoto only knew English words like "middle C" and "again." But when my father said "*ninshin,*" Mr. Sugimoto began to understand. Mommy cried while I stared down at my lap.

Did you know that beneath a doorsill is not the safest place to be when the earth moves? That's what we learned during our emergency drills at Kubasaki High. During an earthquake, you should get far away from everything that makes you feel safe. Your shelves of Nancy Drews, your framed posters of ballet dancers, your daisy mirror—they all become projectiles that could hurt you. When that tiny life quaked inside me, the panic shook our whole house, and I was dropped off at the only place that was safe, far away from all that I loved. Mr. Sugimoto's family let me sleep on a *tatami* mat in a room of oiled paper walls. There I stayed for months, away from flying debris.

I'll tell you a secret. Although I'm fourteen, I still play with dolls. My favorite festival on the island is *Hinamatsuri* because it's Girls' Day and everybody shows off their doll collection. Daddy had bought me all the dolls for a proper display: the emperor and empress, court ladies, musicians, and even servants. But I wasn't allowed to take them with me when they packed me up to live with the Sugimotos. "We'll take them to the States with us," Daddy promised. "You'll have them after you put all this behind you."

They let me hold her for a few minutes on the morning she was born. With her round head and skinny body, she looked like a *kokeshi* doll. She probably knew I would be leaving her in a Japanese orphanage, so the little thing refused to open her eyes. The Sugimotos didn't complain when I wouldn't stop crying. They fed me tea and *mochi* stuffed with sweet bean paste.

During World War II, the sweetest, smartest little Okinawan girls were chosen to be candy stripers on the battlefront. They worked in the airless caves that served as hospitals, picking maggots from the soldiers' festering wounds with chopsticks. Some of them got to take the soldiers' severed, gangrenous limbs and throw them out of the mouth of the caves and into the sea. They were called Princess Lily Girls. They had entered the war the most sheltered and refined girls on the island. But when it was over, those who survived were soiled with knowledge and horror.

Most of the Princess Lily Girls never made it home.

CARTOON
BLUE

MY DESK IS MOLASSES BROWN WITH CLARET UNDER-tones. My chair is Williamsburg blue, tufted with gold buttons. It's on casters so that it rolls easily on the mossy carpet. My phone has three lines; my secretary answers two of them.

The office smells of wood polish and leather, like the inside of a new car. There are high, bright windows that I stare out of all day.

My suit is charcoal and my blouse is ivory with a tasteful rounded collar. My attire hides the troublesome swell of my breasts, the daring rise of my belly. My skin is scent-free, my nails painted clear.

My voice is low, especially when clients are seated in front of my desk. It forces them to lean in to my authority. They rise when I rise, sit when I sit.

The phone rings, and my secretary puts the conference call through. My binder for the closing is black. On the credenza, a gold pendulum swings beneath the clock. Voices are a metronome. The sun rises to a higher yellow.

After an hour on the phone, the buildings outside begin to cast an afternoon shadow. The pages of the binder fan me as I flip through them. On the other side of my door, a paper bag rattles. My secretary is eating at her desk again. There is the burble of a straw. The choking waft of onions drags my morning sickness into the afternoon. I try to concentrate on the voices or on the mantle clock, its gold noose swinging. My stomach starts to roil. Bile rises.

I mute the phone to wretch quickly into the garbage can.

"Are you there?"

"Has she been cut off?"

"No, no, I'm still here," I say, my throat burning. Suddenly, something warm seeps between my legs. My eyes open wide with the fear of loss, but my voice remains steady. The sky is cartoon blue.

The call ends after we schedule the closing. I stand—easy, easy. I walk past the secretary, my thighs slicking. I wonder if she can smell the salty tang of ocean.

The ladies' bathroom has only two stalls. No one dreamed that more than a handful of women would ever work here. The floors are granite tombstones. I sit in a stall, but not for the usual business. Someone might hear me, so I hold my breath while my womb weeps.

Beneath me runs a clotted river. The water is red. The walls are cooling-board brown.

NIGHT COMING

WHY DOESN'T THE KEY FIT?

Nikki hesitated for a second in the early dusk, wondering if she was at the right house—whether the hundred-year-old, rambling Tudor was really where she had lived the past three years. She put down her briefcase and purse, then, looking around nervously, tried the door with both hands.

Nikki had left work early hoping to avoid just this kind of meeting between herself, a locked door, and sundown. The spiral topiaries flanking her front door stood mute. She flinched as a squirrel darted across the damp cedar mulch.

"Damn!" she said, jiggling the key impatiently in the swollen lock. "Damn it all!"

It was stupid, she knew, but suddenly she wanted to cry. Maybe it was the tension that had built up during the desperate rush home to meet Jason, only to see that he hadn't made it there yet, the house disappearing into blackness, the porch cold and unlit.

Maybe it was because she didn't really want to go with him to the Diaspora Ball after all. They went to the benefit for African

American art at the museum every year. She was tired, feeling nauseated. Couldn't they skip it, just this once?

Stemming her burning tears, she gathered her things and clomped to the back of the house, her sleek pumps crushing the brittle leaves in her wake. The motion-sensitive lights along the side of the house blinked on, momentarily holding her startled in their beams.

Entering the back yard, Nikki scanned it quickly: the brick barbeque pit, the teak outdoor furniture, the star-white mums offering a last bloom before frost.

No one was there.

Of course no one's back here, she thought, sniffling courageously. *This neighborhood is safe.*

It was as if the house had been waiting for those magic words. The key turned easily in the back door's lock. Pushing it open with clammy hands, she tread cautiously into the warmth of the kitchen.

"Whew," Nikki said, immediately flipping on the light and locking the door behind her. Putting the briefcase down, she kicked off her shoes and rolled down her panty hose, which, of late, had grown even more confining.

Hungry, she opened the refrigerator. The fare was typical of DINKs—couples with double income, no kids. Leftover Chinese, a bottle of Fat Bastard chardonnay, fruit-on-the-bottom yogurt, Diet Coke.

Nikki eyed the wine but thought better of it, slamming the door. Instead, she took out a box of Cheerios from the pantry and munched to quell her nervous stomach.

"Just a few handfuls," she promised herself, glancing at the clock. "Jason will be home soon and we'll eat dinner at the gala."

She dialed his cell but got his voicemail and hung up. Shrugging, she took her briefcase with her as she wended through the downstairs, turning on all the lights. It was already five thirty. It wasn't like Jason to be late without letting her know where he was—especially lately.

Maybe there's been an accident, she thought. *Maybe he'll never walk again. Maybe he's . . .*

"He's just running late," she said, her voice echoing around the vaulted ceiling. She tried his cell again. No answer.

Placing her briefcase on the coffee table, Nikki plopped onto the leather sofa. Her stomach quivered. Her muscles drew taut like a cat's. She tried to concentrate on the paperwork she'd brought home but stopped after only few minutes. It was futile. The words had no meaning. She felt like an actress, improvising busyness for some invisible audience.

Every once in a while, Nikki touched the back of her neck where her short black hair lay in soft curls against her chai-tea skin. Had she imagined that swift puff of air—a stranger's warm breath?

She thought about the bottle of wine chilling in the refrigerator and was tempted to dash back through the empty house to take a sip. Instead, she picked up the remote, turning on the design channel. But soon she found her attention shifting from flat-screen TV to the neighborhood-security truck outside, its yellow patrol lights splitting the night.

"You'll love it in Detroit," Jason had said about his hometown.

That was five years ago, only weeks after they'd graduated from Emory's business school. Nikki remembered the wide grin on Jason's handsome chestnut face as he'd flapped open his offer letter from General Motors. She'd thrown her arms around him, her heart clutching. Her mediocre grades had left her without similar options.

Nikki's mother had cried when she'd found out her baby girl was moving from Atlanta to Detroit, of all places. Nikki had cried, too, as she'd followed Jason to the Motor City, red-eyed and rudderless.

The newlyweds had sublet a loft in Midtown next to Wayne State University that first summer. Jason had convinced her that it would be a hip place to live, a place where the hookers coexisted with yoga studios, free-trade coffee shops, and trendy resale stores.

For Nikki, Detroit had been her first real adventure. Raised by a black, middle-class Atlanta family, she'd walked on the debutante stage at sixteen and graduated from Spelman College at twenty with a marketing degree—the third generation to attend the historically black women's college. She'd applied to Emory to assuage her parents, who'd kept asking, "What are you going to do now?" Her grades in business school were lackluster, reflecting both her waning interest in the subject and her ambivalence toward graduating. But when she'd met Jason Sykes, a well-heeled Detroiter who had a way with numbers and women, she decided that her investment in graduate school would pay off in one way that she hadn't predicted. They married after their first year.

She'd been immediately seduced by the side of Detroit that never made newspaper headlines. There was the large, tight-knit black upper class, with their galas and vacations on Martha's Vineyard. There were the unbelievably long July days when the sun didn't set until after nine. During her first summer, the city seemed to be in permanent celebration with endless concerts, happy hours, ethnic foods, and festivals.

Maybe Jason was right, Nikki had thought. Detroit just gets a bad rap.

But being from Atlanta, she had no way of knowing that she was experiencing only a seasonal euphoria. As summer turned to fall, a paralyzing darkness encroached upon the city. By December, it seemed to cut the afternoons in two. Nikki found herself leaving the house in the morning and coming home at night without ever seeing the sun. For months on end, the drag of winter circled from gray to black, then back again.

Thankfully, she'd landed a position as a private banker with a suburban boutique bank that first fall. The high-powered job helped rescue her mood. Their second year, they'd bought a house in the exclusive Palmer Woods, the same integrated, ritzy neighborhood where Jason had grown up.

Despite her privileged upbringing, Nikki had a hard time comprehending the wealth that the stately homes in Palmer Woods represented.

"The Archbishop of the Detroit Archdiocese lived there," Jason had said, pointing to a sprawling estate that looked more like a castle than a house. "Then one of the Pistons moved in—can you believe it? And that's the old Fisher mansion."

Fisher, she realized, as in Alfred Fisher, the auto baron. As in one of the many car moguls that blossomed in Detroit in the early twentieth century. Jason was full of stories like that, stories that made her think of the neighborhood of stone mansions, carriage houses, and English gardens as something out of a fairy tale.

"During World War II," he said, "people had to wall off entire sections of their homes to save energy. Neighborhood patrols went around at night and knocked on people's doors if any light was showing through the draped windows. Some people filled their attics with sand in case the roof caught on fire."

When Nikki looked at him quizzically, he added, "The threat of air raids."

Their own house had only three owners, the last of whom had sealed the drafty milk chute and turned the maid's quarters into an exercise room. But it was the back staircase—the one that went from the maid's room to the kitchen—that had given Nikki pause.

"Why would we need that nowadays?" she'd asked as they considered putting down an offer.

Jason had looked at her and shrugged. "I don't know. A secret escape route?"

It had been just a joke, but many nights since, Nikki had lain awake imagining herself scampering down the back stairs to escape an intruder. Or worse, an intruder creeping up the hidden staircase to where they lay sleeping.

Nikki had quickly filled the den, dining room, and master bedroom with furniture from mail-order catalogs—the hard-working couple barely had time for grocery shopping, much less interior decorating. They left the rest of the sprawling Tudor empty. On weekends, she and Jason spent Sundays trolling for antiques to accent the other rooms.

But deep down, Nikki worried that escape would be harder when weighed down by useless things.

Outside, a car pulled up in the driveway, the headlights forming prison-bar shadows through the blinds.

Jason! Nikki thought. But before she could get up, the car backed out, then headed in the opposite direction down the winding, elm-lined street.

She sighed heavily, hating herself for being so clingy. It was nearly six thirty according to the dull, green read-out on the cable box. *I guess I should get ready,* she thought, sighing.

Her footfalls creaked on the refinished maple stairs. She laughed at herself for wondering—if only for a second—whether the sounds were coming from someone else lurking inside the old house.

In the bathroom, she took off her St. John knitted suit. She couldn't help but notice the slight bulge of her stomach, which made her self-conscious even though it was easily hidden beneath her straight-cut jackets.

After running a bath, she sat upright in the claw-foot tub, with only the sounds of the settling house to keep her company. She thought about turning on the television in the master bedroom or putting on some Miles Davis, but what if someone tried to break in and she couldn't hear?

Jason will be home soon, she thought. The warm water was like a baptism. She breathed in the lavender aroma of the suds and let her shoulders relax.

When had she become a woman afraid to stay alone in her own house? It was the news. The constant stories of carjackings and murders. The endless stream of black men in mug shots, or bent low with their hands cuffed, being pushed into the back of police cruisers.

No, it wasn't just the news—it was the way the different social classes bumped up against each other in Detroit. In Atlanta, this house—all five thousand square feet of it—wouldn't come complete with poor neighbors.

Nikki added more hot water to her bath and closed her eyes. She remembered her first Halloween in Palmer Woods. How she'd gone and bought three bags of candy even though she'd seen very few children in the neighborhood.

That Halloween had been particularly cold, and she'd wondered how the children were going to show off their angel's wings and Superman capes if they were bundled up like Eskimos. She'd just come home from work and had barely finished a bowl of pumpkin soup before the doorbell rang.

She'd put on her witch's hat and run to the door, expecting to see tiny tots hollering, "Trick or treat!" But more often than not, there were adults and teenagers, most with only a half-cocked attempt at a costume—the stark, white face paint of the "Dead Presidents," or a terrifying Freddie Krueger mask—holding out a pillowcase for candy. They came in droves all night, tumbling out of buses and church vans, hungry adults vying with children for the best candy.

The enormity of it shocked and depressed her. As she opened the door, some of them peeked inside. "You have a nice house," they'd say and she'd blush, Marie Antoinette doling out her little pieces of cake.

Within an hour after sunset, she'd run out of candy and had started combing the kitchen for bags of chips, apples, anything. She finally closed the door and turned off all of the lights, trembling. And still, the footsteps came.

That was Detroit. A city where there was no place to hide.

"Nikki? Nikki!" Her husband's voice came suddenly from the front stairs, his keys jangling in his hand.

Nikki felt a wash of relief. "I'm in the tub getting ready. Where were you?"

"On an international conference call—couldn't get away to call you. Sorry."

Just like that, there he was grinning in the doorway, his teal silk tie setting off his russet complexion. "Is that what you're wearing?" he asked, his eyes lingering on the bubbles glistening against her amber skin.

In his presence, the noises of the house silenced themselves. Her fears shriveled.

"Stop playing," she said. "Get dressed."

There's no such thing as a little bit pregnant.

Nikki was surprised at how true the old adage was, how completely pregnancy had changed everything, even though she was only twelve weeks and barely showing. Even now, as Jason helped her into her vintage Mouton coat, she felt a tip in the balance between them, a perplexing reliance upon him that she hadn't felt in their five-year marriage.

"Careful," he said, tucking her into the Cadillac.

Nikki noticed, too, how her own senses had become heightened. As they walked up the marble steps to the Detroit Institute of Arts, the cold spotlight of the moon caused her to squint. She could almost hear the brittle tree limbs overhead clacking in the autumn wind. Jason's cologne was suddenly overpowering. Was there something distant in his touch as he guided her by the elbow into the Diaspora Ball?

The surprise of her pregnancy wasn't helping. When she had emerged from the bathroom crying with joy, Jason had held her too tightly and whispered in her ear, "Are you sure?" He'd been full of reasons why they shouldn't have a baby: He traveled too much. They didn't have enough savings for a nanny and private school. They'd just bought the house.

Nikki had listened to his rational arguments and smiled. At least he was thinking like a father even if he suddenly wasn't sure he wanted to be one, she'd thought. Maybe what he needed was time to get used to the idea.

Since then, the baby had floated between them in a sea of silence.

"Julie!" came Jason's greeting as he planted the customary kiss on an acquaintance's cheek. "Julie, you remember my wife? Nikki . . ."

Nikki smiled and offered a limp handshake. There was an effort at conversation—the Pistons, the mayoral election, the coming auto show—then on to another couple. Sipping club soda with a lime twist, Nikki soon found herself wandering away from Jason's salesman-like energy. She needed to breathe.

She found herself where she always ended up whenever she visited the art institute, even when she came there for Thursday-night jazz or Sunday brunch with Bach: the *Nkonde*, a nail figure from the Congo.

It was like no other artifact in the African collection. Standing nearly four feet tall and carved out of ebony, its features were oddly un-African—a jutting chin, a sharp nose, and bony cheeks. Against the palette of the smooth, smoky wood were the figure's half-moon eyes, as white and dazed as those painted on a sarcophagus. Nikki hadn't noticed the cowrie-shell belly button before. Tonight, it seemed to gape with rawness, as if the figure had just been yanked from an umbilical cord.

What always drew her to the *Nkonde* was its torso, jabbed with rusted nails, screws, and blades. According to the museum placard, when two parties reached an agreement, they'd drive a nail into its body to seal the deal. If anyone broke the promise, the *Nkonde's* spirit would punish him.

The *Nkonde's* body was a garment of promises, spikes sticking horribly from its chest, belly, shoulders, and even its chin. The figure's mouth was partially open in punctured surprise. Nikki gazed at it in horrified fascination, wondering how the parties had decided where to impale the figure to memorialize their contracts. What were they doing now, the proof of their promises locked behind a glass case in a museum?

The din of the party faded as Nikki stood there, entranced. She was suddenly aware of the low-grade nausea that was her constant companion. Her head started to swim. It seemed like the figure wanted to tell her something.

Then came the sound—a man's familiar laughter echoing in the empty exhibit hall.

"What *else* do you want me to do to you?"

Low murmurs. A woman's muffled giggles.

"Jason?" Nikki whispered, as the *Nkonde* stared back, eyes hard white.

Her heart began to pound. Nikki spun around, but she was alone in the gallery. Had she imagined the voices? She fought to tamp down the bile gathering at her throat. She fled back to the crowd, hoping to make an escape. She was nearly to the door when someone grabbed her arm.

"Nikki? I didn't know you were here!"

It was her sorority sister, Terry Hines, dressed, as always, in shades of pink and green.

"Hey, Terry," Nikki managed foggily.

"Girl, are you OK?"

Nikki blinked twice. *Try to get it together.* "I—I'm pregnant."

As soon as the words left her lips, she regretted the slip. Detroit was a small, big town. People were constantly cross-pollinating. Gossip took root quickly.

"What!" Terry shrieked, her garnet lips shimmering against her dark honey skin. Then, lowering her voice conspiratorially, she asked, "How far along are you? Do you need to sit down?"

Before she could answer, Jason was at her side. "There you are!" he said, exasperated. "I was wondering where you'd wandered off to!" He sidled up to her, lovingly planting a kiss on her cheek.

"My God, Jason, Nikki just told me!" gushed Terry, not catching the look of foreboding in Nikki's eyes.

Jason glanced from Terry's exuberant face to Nikki's miserable one, sizing up the awkward pause.

"The baby?" Terry prompted.

Jason was taken aback. "Oh!" he said, smiling uneasily. "Yeah! Imagine me—a dad!"

"We're not really telling people yet," Nikki said. "It's still early, you know. . . ."

Terry's eyes grew large and she covered her mouth as if to cap a secret. "Of course," she said. "But I just know that everything will be fine."

"I'd better get you home," Jason said. "You look a little pale."

Nikki nodded, letting him lead her toward the door, his hand firm around her waist. Her body went limp against his, seeking forgiveness.

Outside, the night air had turned frosty. "It slipped," Nikki said finally, as they waited for their car.

Jason nodded but said nothing. As they rode home, she glared at the sights along Woodward, the strange people with their nightshade business, shivering in the cold.

Jason noticed her trembling and turned up the heat. The fan only blew the freezing air harder and she reached up to close the vents. She could feel his eyes on her, but he said nothing to lighten the mood. The moon, yellowing as it rose, followed them home.

His silence humiliated her, and she wondered how he'd managed to turn the tables so quickly. Wasn't it he who'd just backed another woman against a display case and fondled her? Wasn't it he who'd suddenly been unable to come home on time like he used to, who always left her waiting, who wouldn't return her calls?

When they arrived home, he walked around to her side of the car to help her out. On the porch, he was about to put the keys in the lock, but instead he turned and said, "I don't want a baby."

He stared at her, his eyes accusing her of ruining everything. But she stared back, her feet planted and steady, the queasiness fading into resolve.

"I do," she said back, the shivering suddenly ceasing. "I do."

He lowered his eyes. For a long moment, he didn't speak. "It's cold out here," he said finally. "Let's talk inside."

He leaned to put the key in the door, but like a dark invitation, it swung open by itself. His eyes shot her a question: "Didn't you lock the door?" But it was too late.

Inside the house, the night moved.

MOURNING
CHAIR

I WISH THIS SEAT WERE A ROCKING CHAIR. THEN I COULD pretend that this is just another long night in the nursery, you burning hot in my arms.

But it's not a rocking chair and you're not in my arms. I'm sitting in your grandmother's chair. The faded blue one with the overstuffed cushions of worn brocade.

You once said that you wished we'd throw this chair out—that it was embarrassing. Especially after that time you brought that boy home, the one from the football team who made you look like a matchstick in comparison. Your father sat him in this chair and grilled him before your first date.

I've moved the chair to the living-room window, so that I can have a view of the street through the sheers. The only time I've left this chair all night was to check the clock at least an hour ago. Or maybe it was only ten minutes ago. Or maybe I've been sitting in a chair by a window for seventeen years, since the day you were born.

All evening, I've been rising eagerly each time I see headlights cutting the darkness. I fall back into the sorrowful cushions whenever the cars slow and pick some other anxious mother's driveway.

But I'm becoming smarter, like a woman on the maternity ward who's roused only by the sound of her own baby's cry. I'll know when the right car turns the corner. The knot in my stomach will suddenly unfurl.

The street is long-silent. I have begun to prepare myself for the worst. What if the next car that comes around the corner is a cruiser? I have rehearsed my description of you:

My daughter is easy to recognize, officer. She has a scar by her left eye—a tangle with Ginger, her moody cat. She has her father's high, caramel cheeks that always make her look like she's just finished laughing. The gap in her teeth—passed down to her from the tribes of West Africa—has been closed with silver braces. And she has her grandmother's deep gray eyes. The same grandmother who watches over me now, as I sit in her blue chair.

My daughter is easy to recognize, officer. She's the one with her heart beating in my pocket.

I shift in the chair and take another sip of tepid, oily coffee. I have to use the bathroom, but instead I begin to pray for forgiveness. Maybe my sinful thoughts that night so long ago is why God has put me in this chair by the window tonight, with you out there somewhere, lost to me.

That night, I was full of you. Full to popping. Nine months pregnant and a whole week overdue. I sat weeping in this very chair for God to take both of us right there and then. I didn't want to live, and I didn't want to leave you behind. I was tired of the double habitation of my body, the split duties of my soul. I wanted to be complete again, alone within myself. Whole. I wanted my old appetites; my small, unswollen feet; my easy greeting of the day. You took those things from me and replaced them with unknowable fears, unsoothable pain, insatiable dread.

I prayed all night as I paced by the cabinet of poisonous things, by the drawer of sharpened knives. I thought about throwing myself down the stairs or starting the car in the garage. Somehow, I held on to my own life while your grandmother's spirit held on to yours.

In the morning, I woke up in this chair, exhausted and full of shame. The next hour, the pains came. You'd smelled the danger and gotten out.

Daughter.

They weren't tears of joy that I cried the moment you arrived, mewling and fetal with your lips already painted red. They were tears of relief that the waiting was over. We would spend the rest of our days learning how to live apart.

Here comes a car. My throat clutches. This is the one. Four houses away, the driver cuts the engine and turns off the headlights. The car coasts to our driveway.

The car door opens and out you tumble. You giggle as your date pulls you into a drunken hug, gives you a deep kiss.

You push him back and look around guiltily. You know that I am always here, always watching. He grabs your hand and leads you to the steps. I want to throw open the door and damn you for your selfishness.

The front door creaks open and I hear footsteps. I have been waiting for this moment all night, but now I am afraid of how much I hate you. I hide behind sleep.

"Ma?"

I feel your presence, electric. You used to be mine. Now, you're someone else's. I smell perfume, smoke, and fresh mouthwash.

There is a heaviness over me, a warm cloak. You have covered me with a blanket. You kiss the top of my head gently. I want to hold you, pummel you, smell the sweet curve of your neck.

"I'm home," you whisper.

CEILING

THE LAW FIRM WAS NO PLACE FOR A WOMAN, LAW review or otherwise. He said as much, sucking the end of his pipe, eyes gazing past his glasses to her tender breasts. She tried not to shrivel beneath his stare. She felt faint, like a rice-paddy woman bent in muddy water as a baby hardened her womb.

"Maternity leave?" he repeated, considering her quietly, a problem to be solved. Pipe smoke curled to the ceiling—a halo of power. His tie was burqa blue and lemon yellow, a robin's egg cracked open, yolk running. He leaned forward and knocked his pipe on the crystal ashtray, filling the room with the linger of fire. She was nothing more than a useless bride, crossed legs as brown as firewood ready to be doused, life going up in saffron flames.

"If you wanted to have babies," he said, smiling gently, "why did you go to law school?"

ORIGINS OF SACRIFICE

FOR MORE THAN AN HOUR, KATE WAITED TENSELY FOR her husband to arrive home from work. She jostled their fussy newborn as the teenage sitter watched her pace. Maybe Jim had forgotten that he had promised to take Kate out—just a few hours away from the mewling child, the toe-curling pain of breast-feeding, the smell of sour milk and dirty diapers.

Maybe he was holed up in a meeting or on a conference call and couldn't get away. Maybe he was joining a coworker for Dewar's on the rocks, or holding the hand of a distraught client at a bar, or working too closely with his secretary before going home to a shapeless wife who was always full of tears.

But suddenly, there he was, pulling up in the driveway. Jim walked up the sidewalk slack shouldered, hauling his briefcase like an anvil. Kate thrust the baby into the sitter's arms and threw open the door, as anxious and grateful to be outside as a full-bladdered puppy. He hugged her and placed apologetic kisses on the curve of her neck. "Ready?" he asked. Kate was happy that he did not want to sit a minute first, or change his clothes or glance at the paper.

She scurried off like a sixteen-year-old escaping the farm in a beat-up Mustang. It was so good to be out that Kate hardly minded at all when "dinner and a movie" turned out to be Wendy's and the latest Nicolas Cage film.

"We'll get dessert after," Jim consoled.

The movie didn't end until almost eleven. Kate was full from the greasy burger and buttery popcorn, but her mouth still watered for something more. The smooth, sweet, creamy taste of a promise remembered.

"You look nice," Jim said.

He hadn't told her she looked nice when they had started out on their date. Or even as they stood in the shambling ticket line. Instead, he said it now, in the dark as they drove home, not even taking his eyes off the road. Kate put her hand on her stomach—a habit from nine months of pregnancy—to point out, in case he hadn't noticed, that she was slimmer now. Minus a whole six pounds, eight ounces.

In the darkness, Kate stared hard at the side of Jim's face. He was as handsome as ever, the lights from oncoming traffic painting a ribbon of light across his deep-set eyes and friendly brow. She marveled at how she had arrived at the other end of childbirth a stranger even to herself. But he was unchanged since the baby, except more plugged into work. He kept promising her that if he played his cards right, he'd be up for a promotion. Then they could think about a bigger house.

Jim steered with one hand, driving into the quiet evening, preoccupied with important things. Kate stared jealously at how easy driving was for him—like an extension of breathing. Because she had been put on bed rest—and then had a C-section—Kate hadn't been able to drive for months. She tried to remember that feeling of absolute, one-handed control.

"I liked the movie," Kate said, and he laughed amiably. They both knew she had hated the movie, all those cars crashing and buildings exploding. But she had liked the act of pushing money across the counter at the concession stand, sitting in a theater full of strangers, being out on a weeknight.

Jim yawned deeply, and Kate took it personally. Did he have to make such a big show of being tired? Had he forgotten all about the promised dessert? She closed her eyes and imagined tiramisu. A lemon-curd tart topped with glazed berries. A frothy espresso and candlelight. Warm Baileys even though she was still breast-feeding. Maybe she expected too much. It served her right for getting her hopes up. She should have been satisfied with the Frosty.

Anyway, Kate told herself, it was better to get back home and check on the baby and the new sitter. Jim had to get up early. Plus, there would be feedings every two or three hours. She needed rest more than she needed empty calories.

"I didn't get the promotion," Jim said, almost to himself.

Kate exhaled sadly and reached for her husband's hand. She held it tenderly, giving him permission to end the night now, to head home. Jim gave her a grateful glance, but Kate didn't return it. Instead, she watched the headlights swallow the white lines in the road.

IN THE
GINZA

BOBBIE JEAN PUSHED THE STROLLER THROUGH THE crowded market and silently rehearsed her textbook Japanese. *"Ohayō"*—pronounced just like Ohio—for "good morning." *"Gomen"* for "I'm sorry." *"Dōmo arigatō,"* lots of syllables for a simple thanks.

She was elegant and chestnut-skinned, her thick hair pinned in a French roll, her hands kid-gloved. No one would recognize who she was beneath her polished cotton dress with sharp darts and perfect pleats: a country girl whose childhood had been crowded with big Virginia pines and bigger dreams.

She had quickly completed her mission in college—to find a husband in the first year—and left behind the backwoods town that always smelled of pig shit and sawdust. Now here she was, the wife of an airman first-class, raising her brand-new baby in postwar Japan.

Bobbie Jean leaned over the sturdy pram and adjusted her daughter's pink summer blanket. It had seemed like a good idea that morning to take a stroll off the base into downtown Fukuoka. But the market air was thick with dried squid and seaweed, and the push of women with their wicker baskets made the pram feel hulking and pretentious. The Japanese *okaasan*s never used strollers. Their babies were always lashed to their backs, even as they hunched in the rice paddies.

"Maybe we should go home now," Bobbie Jean said to the dozing child, who began to suckle the air at the sound of her mother's voice.

Bobbie Jean had just turned toward home when she caught the smell of roasted sweet potatoes, their syrup dripping onto the hot coals. For a second, her stomach quivered, hungry for the familiar.

She steered the stroller toward a group of kimonoed old women, their heads wrapped in blue-and-white scarves. "*Ichi, dōzo.*" Bobbie held up a one-fingered request while bowing slightly.

The women tittered toothlessly. The plump one put down her paper fan and went to claim a potato from the iron pot where they sat cooling.

"You baby-chan?" the other woman asked, peering into the stroller.

Bobbie Jean moved the delicate blanket so that the women could take a peek. Her little girl had barely been six pounds at birth. Even now, three months later, she was still as fragile as porcelain, her skin pale against the dark curl of her silky hair.

The Japanese women drew in deep breaths and Bobbie smiled proudly. Indeed, her baby was beautiful. But instinct made Bobbie Jean's skin prickle as the old women kept pointing at the pram and debating. The plump one spat with finality into a tin can by her wooden chair. "You baby-chan?" she asked Bobbie Jean again. This time the question felt like a cross-examination.

"*Hai,*" said Bobbie, putting her hand over her breast. "My baby-chan."

"Ahhhh," the women nodded at each other knowingly and began to discuss something again, pointing first at Bobbie, then at the sleeping child.

Irritated, Bobbie dug into her coin purse, then held out some bronze yen coins.

The women ignored her, clucking like hens. Tears began to rise instinctively, but Bobbie Jean resisted the urge to back away. This wasn't the rural South, where uppityness could cost her life. This was postwar Japan, and her husband was protecting both his country and theirs. She had every right to be in the ginza buying a roasted sweet potato.

"You got GI?" One of the women crept closer. Her teeth were rotted nubs and her skin was tanned and leathery. She pointed to the baby, then to Bobbie: "You got white GI?"

Bobbie Jean stepped back, understanding the accusation. Her daughter's pale cheeks and cat-slick hair were scarlet letters. Even here, halfway around the world, a decent colored woman was easily taken for a whore.

Without answering, she paid quickly and took the warm yam. The smell was suddenly sickly sweet. Until then, Bobbie Jean hadn't realized how much it reminded her of home.

HOME FOR THE HOLIDAYS

"STILL MAD?" RASHAUN'S SLEEPY VOICE CAME FROM THE passenger's seat.

"Nope," Renee said tersely. She was still mad but didn't want to talk about it. She'd rather make the last hour of their trip from Detroit to Baltimore pleasant. Instead of casting a plastic smile at Rashaun, she focused intently on the darkness, guiding their blue Ford with plates that said "MTRCTY" quietly down I-80.

"If you're not mad, why are your lips still tight?" Rashaun never knew when to leave well enough alone. He sat up in his seat, yawning loudly.

"You're gonna wake them up," Renee complained, glancing into the back seat where four-year-old Sydney and her two-year-old brother, Marcus, snoozed in their car seats.

"Where are we?" Rashaun asked, squinting into the night. The car's solitary headlights made darts of snow appear like magic.

"I don't know. Hagerstown, maybe."

"Maryland? Jeez, how long have I been asleep? I gotta pee."

"Can't you wait until we get there? You're worse than the kids."

Rashaun sulked. "Yes, Mother."

"Fuck you." *This is it*, Renee thought. *After we make nice at Mom's this Christmas, no more pretending. It's over.*

Renee squinted through tears and adjusted the rearview mirror. There was a car behind them—maybe a truck—with lights that seared her retinas. Ella Fitzgerald's voice singing "Baby It's Cold Outside" lilted from the radio. Rashaun sang along. Renee's heart quieted. His voice was like the sky whispering her name. Like wind lifting a kite.

When the song was over, the tension in the car had shifted. "You want me to drive?" he asked tenderly.

Renee hesitated. "That truck has been following us," she said instead of saying that she was sorry. "For the past fifteen minutes, every time I slow down, he slows down. When I change lanes, so does he."

Rashaun turned off the radio. "Why didn't you say something?"

Their car was awash with light as the truck suddenly gunned forward in the thickening snow, flanking their little Ford. The truck waffled close to Rashaun's door, then swerved back into its own lane.

"Jesus!" Rashaun whispered. "Drunk motherfuckers!"

That's when Renee saw their faces, white and laughing. Instinctively, she reached into the back seat and touched Sydney's warm leg, then did what her heart begged her not to do.

She slowed down.

The truck beside them slowed, too. The driver rolled down the window. "Hey, niggers! Go back to the Monkey City where you belong!"

"Ignore them, baby," Rashaun said. "Just keep going."

Renee sped up. The truck sped up and fishtailed in front of them. "Careful—they might stop short," said Rashaun. He put his hand on Renee's thigh, tethering her. She could hear Marcus's tiny snores in the back seat.

Out of the night, a road sign appeared, its arms wide open: "Next Rest Stop 1 Mile." Silently, Renee weighed the options. What if the truck followed them to the rest stop? What if no other cars were there to help them? Renee imagined the police on her mother's porch on Christmas Eve, bearing the horrible news.

As the exit appeared, the truck zoomed past it, but not before a man leaned from the passenger side and threw something. An open can of beer crashed against the windshield, sudsing the car. Renee shrieked as their Ford three-sixtyed on the icy ramp. The children woke screaming as the car skidded to a stop. Rashaun unbuckled his seat belt and leapt into the back seat. Clutching the children tightly, he kissed them into calmness.

Panting, Renee slowly guided the car to the rest-stop parking lot. She parked, jumped out, and started walking in the snow.

Behind her, she heard the passenger car door open. "Stay here— Daddy's got to pee." There were footsteps, then a hand took hers. Rashaun pulled her stiff body into his arms.

"It's OK, baby," he said. She felt her legs buckle as she sobbed into his shoulder. "We're safe now," he whispered. "You and I . . . we're going to be OK."

FIFTEEN ITEMS OR LESS

AFTER LEAVING WORK LATE AND PAYING A SMALL FOR-
tune to spring the kids from daycare, Jackie realized she had no milk
at home. Or cereal or applesauce.

It was nearly seven and the snow had started up again as she
pulled into the Sav-a-Lot. "I want Double Stuf Oreos!" four-year-old
Robin said, skipping ahead toward the cookie aisle. Chase, just entering his terrible twos, tried to lunge after his sister.

It was all Jackie could do to corral Robin and cram Chase into
the seat of a grocery basket without losing her cool. "We're getting in,
and we're getting out," she declared.

Racing through the aisles, she scanned for what she needed and
what she was going to need soon. When she was done, Jackie counted
the items in her basket. Eighteen. Twenty if you counted the two-for-
one boxes of cereal as separate items.

"Mommy, why can't we get the Double Stuf Oreos?" Robin persisted, tugging on the front of Jackie's V-neck sweater, exposing her
dingy bra.

Furious, Jackie batted away her daughter's hand. Robin began to
whimper, and that meant that Chase was going to start up, too. Jackie

gave Robin the evil eye and she piped down, wiping her nose on the sleeve of her coat. Jackie ignored her, hoping it was just grocery-store dramatics and not another cold.

At the checkout, Chase twisted in the cart and grabbed the bright pink box of tampons out of the basket. "Thanks, buddy!" Jackie said with fake sweetness.

"No!" he screamed, refusing to let go.

"Put it down," Jackie said behind bared teeth, like an angry ventriloquist. "I mean it!"

"Can we get some McDonald's?" Robin begged.

"Fifteen items or less, ma'am," the cashier said, pointing to the sign above the register.

Jackie glanced up, her eyes ablaze. "You've got to be kidding," she said, snatching the box of tampons from Chase and throwing it on the conveyor belt. The cashier snatched the box and scanned it, then threw it at the bag boy.

Chase began to scream. Jackie took a box of Frosted Flakes from the scanned items and shoved it at him.

"Can we, Mom?" Robin persisted.

"That'll be forty-nine fifty."

Jackie pulled out her wallet, blood pulsing loudly at her temples. She counted out her money slowly, as if that would make more materialize. "Forty, forty-five . . ." she said, then halted.

"Five more," the cashier wiggled her fingers impatiently.

Chase was now screaming as he pummeled the box of cereal. Jackie's legs began to wobble. She could hear all of the silent judgments: *Why doesn't she shut those kids up? She's probably on food stamps. Another single mom popping out children she can't afford.*

"I got it." A woman bundled in a gray wool coat leaned over and handed the cashier a five. She smiled at Jackie and patted Robin's head. "It's dinnertime. That was the hardest part of the day when I was bringing up my kids."

"I want a Happy Meal," Robin said, pouting.

"Thank you," Jackie said, pulling on her coat despite the fact that she was sweating. "You don't know how much I appreciate this."

Outside, the downy snow muffled the night. Still clutching the Frosted Flakes, Chase sucked cold air in dry heaves. Jackie mined her keys from the bottom of her purse, then pushed the remote to unlock her dented SUV.

"Get in and buckle up," she commanded Robin as she lifted the trunk to put in the groceries.

Out of nowhere, there was the smell of must and urine. A man hovered by her open trunk, wearing only a flannel shirt, soiled jeans, and tennis shoes. His matted hair was frosted by the new snow.

Was he going to take her purse? Kill her in front of her children? Steal the car with Robin strapped in the backseat?

"I need a dollar for the bus," he said.

"I—I don't have any money," she said. It was the truth, but with her fat toddler in the cart, bags of groceries, and a decent car, she knew it sounded like a lie. The man stepped closer. His smell was sharp and threatening. The dullness of his eyes dared her not to scream. He reached toward Chase. Jackie grabbed her son while the man snatched the box of Frosted Flakes.

He fled into the night, the falling snow erasing his footsteps.

SOFT
LANDING

I.

ONE NIGHT, AS I LAY AWAKE IN THE SWELTERING DARK-ness, the stars called me back to the beginning. I went outside and gazed skyward where Orion hung low and the Milky Way dangled within reach. A current of evolution stirred; suddenly I was certain of my fetal wings.

Pressing my bare soles against the damp ground, I angled my crooked spine and pushed up on swollen knees. I was aloft.

I should have been ashamed, a tiny woman of a certain age, allowing the world to see her nethers as she soared toward the antique moon. But no. The thrill of the evening breeze lifting my thin gown only made me laugh. My center of gravity shifted; the years molted away like useless feathers.

Circling over all that I knew, I saw the sorrows and joys blink-ing below me like runway lights. My slack biceps became an aileron, my calcified trunk a fuselage. The air rushed over the hump of my back, creating lift. The vertigo of natural forces. The glide of ancient impulses. It was as easy as dreaming.

Night after night, I took to the air. Sometimes, I could sense a ripple in the currents, the way a familiar room feels after a stranger has lingered. Then I knew I was part of an invisible flock. There were others who had remembered the time before time, when we all had wings.

II.

The gate for my plane was at the end of concourse B. I made my way slowly on thick Birkenstocks, bewildered by all the rushing to nowhere. The hoard of travelers parted around me, a stream flowing around a heavy stone.

I arrived at my gate with forty-five minutes to spare. Resting in the boarding area, I picked them out easily. The splotched man with goggle-like sunglasses who wouldn't stop tilting his face toward the sun. The woman wearing a billowy, blue muumuu, fat flaps beneath her arms. The somber gentleman in a wheelchair with reedy legs and owl eyes. The squat woman with the broad shoulders, whose grandchildren ambled behind her in a V.

When the plane arrived, these were the people who boarded first—all of us hollow-boned creatures who required extra time. My seatmate was a twitchy man with a sharp nose and eagle-black eyes. As the engines ignited, he gave me a dentured smile.

An hour into the flight, I was jostled awake by the turbulence. I glanced at the man beside me, resisting the urge to grab his hand. It was then that I noticed his feet planted on the floor, legs rigid, and I could tell that he was doing the same thing I was doing—pressing his soles against the metal floor, ready to leap.

When the engine spit fire over the Rockies, my heart stuttered against my ribcage. Outside of the window, the sun spilled vermillion. Behind us, a plume of dark smoke.

Fasten your seat belts and place your heads down on your knees.
Women screamed; men sobbed into their hands. As the plane dove,
the cabin walls groaned. Luggage shifted in the holds. Strangers
united in prayer.

My seatmate, however, was unafraid. Against instructions, we
unfastened our seat belts, knotted our hands together, and waited.
Two-hundred bodies thundered into the sky. The air snatched our
voices. People fell like rain.

But those of us who remembered threw open our arms and flew.

SOMETHING FALLS IN THE NIGHT

JUMP UP, RUN SWIFTLY OVER THE HARDWOOD FLOOR. Don't worry about your thin gown or your ungirded body beneath. Creep into your son's room and pinch him from his dreams. Greet his frightened eyes with the fury of survival. Clamp your hand over his mouth to cork a scream.

Listen to sounds crashing downstairs. Lift the window sash to the sting of winter. Poise your child on the ledge, and push.

In the nursery, the baby cries. Dash to her side before she gives you away. Downstairs, the ransacking pauses; the living-room curio hangs midtilt. They must have heard her little sobs.

A boot breaches the steps. Quickly, you lift the baby, crush her head to your breast to stifle her cries. Do you dive into the bathtub and flatten yourself against the porcelain, praying that the shower curtain is bulletproof? Do you roll with the child into the darkness beneath the bed? Cower behind the door armed with a golf club? Huddle in the bottom of the hall closet?

Or do you stand in the middle of the room, await the shadows in the doorway, and fight?

Jump up, run swiftly over the creaky floors. You are fully dressed. You go first to the baby's room, where she is dreaming about the warm suckle of your breast. You lift her rudely, and her arms and legs startle. She opens her mouth to scream so deeply, no sound comes out. You swaddle her in the thick down of her cradle blanket, open the window, and throw her into the snow.

Downstairs, there is the creak of a stranger's foot on the bottom step. Blood pounds loudly in your ears. You can barely hear your son call, "Mommy?"

The footsteps come faster. You dart down the hall to your son's room, scoop him from the bed. His body is supple and ready for a hug, but you spit "Shut up," through gritted teeth. He is shocked silent. You open the window just as the knob on his bedroom door turns. You dangle him into the night. You ignore the question in his eyes as you let go.

Jump up, run swiftly over the creaky hardwood floors. You have been sitting up in the chair, waiting with a pistol in your lap. You slip by the bedroom door where your son sleeps in his footie pajamas. You glance at the room where your infant daughter shivers.

Downstairs, someone is talking loudly. Drawers slam and dishes shatter. You take one step on the stairs, which groan with the weight of fear. The house goes silent. Someone is listening. A shadow lengthens at the bottom of the stairs. The bedroom door opens and your son says, "Mommy?" just as you pull the trigger.

Jump up, run swiftly into the winter night. Look back at your sweet house, with its Williamsburg shutters and stained-glass door. Upstairs, your children sleep without dreaming.

You are fully dressed, but you have forgotten your shoes. You wait shivering at a bus stop. When it arrives in the darkness, it is nearly empty. You board, your feet numb and clumsy. There is a woman dozing against the window. The bus jostles her little boy awake. When he looks at you, he shrinks and whines, "Mommy?"

You point the gun and shoot.

LEFTOVERS

THE SUN WARMS THE WINDOWPANES AS I LINGER ON the edge of a dream. Downstairs, I can hear Cassie squealing like a piglet and Brandon is not using his inside voice. I should go and see where David is. He's probably on the phone with the office. They can't make a double-sided copy without calling him fifty times.

But no, I will lie here for a minute more and drift in solitude. This is the blessing of illness. If I tilt my face toward the window and close my eyes, I can imagine myself on a sugar-white beach, my soul wafting skyward on shimmering light.

The Egyptian cotton sheets cover half of my body, exposing one lonely breast, half of a sunken stomach, the bald triangle of my pubis, one sturdy thigh, one jogger's calf. I loll in the bed, resplendent. My nudity is neither sexy nor fecund. Finally, I am neither a lover's playground nor a child's milk bar.

Cassie is now wailing. I should get up and straighten things out. Have the children had their naps today?

Beside my bed sits a bright Talavera bowl and a thin spoon. David and I bought these dishes on our honeymoon in the Yucatán. When was the last time that I ate? When will David get off of the cell phone, quiet the children, and remember that he has a bedridden wife upstairs?

A woman sick is a woman forgotten.

I need to go to the bathroom. I can't bear shattering the sun-warmed peace with the sound of my own voice, so I don't call for help. Instead, I rise against the nausea and claw along the walls like a blind woman.

I sit on the cool porcelain, cupping my remaining, doleful breast as if it were a fallen nestling. The petroleum smell of the plastic Sponge-Bob shower curtain makes me gag, so I breathe through my mouth. I can't believe I'm alone in the bathroom, without Cassie sputtering on my lap or Brandon jumping up and down on the bathroom scale. I never figured out how to be the authority in their lives while hunkering on the toilet with my pants around my ankles. How do you wipe with dignity?

For now, this is no longer my problem—it's David's. He won't anguish over it like I do. He'll just close the door against the children and chance that they won't hurt themselves—or each other—while he's on the toilet.

The kids have gone silent. David must have finally put on a movie so that he can finish some work. Part of me wants him to take this moment to check on me. To find me heroically standing up on my own. To scold me while he takes my arm and leads me gingerly back to bed. I want him to tuck me in and bring me tea.

But there's another part of me. The part that has started to live again after facing so much death. The part of me that hopes that he stays tied up with work and the kids long after dinner, long after the eleven o'clock news. Long after I am already asleep.

I can't bear to feel the obligatory weight of David sliding between the sheets. I don't want to be pinned beneath his leaden arm, my side filling with tingles, my lungs fighting for air.

I long for just one night without his unspoken yearning for the womanhood I have lost. I want one night when I can wrap myself in my own arms and revel in the blessing of all that I have left.

ON THE RIM

A TRIO OF LAZY BURROS CLOMPED ALONG THE LIP OF A
sheer crevasse, each entrusted with one of my three boys. I was the
last one in the mule train, unable to reach the children should one of
the gray, splay-eared animals tumble. My heart pounded a constant
prayer. But for the boys, the danger enlivened the adventure. They
hooted like television cowpokes, then listened as the canyon threw
back their voices.

The mountains around us ribboned red and gray. Dust clouded
the trail ahead where the kids—eleven, eight, and a contrary seven—
wended their way down toward the falls. I looked to our Havasupai
guide, with his cedar skin and grim mouth, to ask him if he really
thought it was safe to let the boys ride so far ahead. But then I
remembered the way his tribe made a living—escorting doughy tour-
ists and their dimpled children down the side of the canyon day after
day—and I held my tongue.

Brian, if he were still here with us, would have laughed at me for
being such a worrywart. *Of course it's safe,* he would have said, planting a kiss on my cheek. *You don't make money by spilling your customers
down the sides of cliffs.*

By noon, we reached the falls of the people of the blue-green water. The boys whooped and splashed in. A rotting log had fallen into the cool basin and they lassoed it for a float. They waved for me to join them, but I could no longer trust places where my feet didn't touch the ground.

They floated happily without me, deeper and deeper into the tourmaline water. I shielded my eyes and strained in the direction of their laughter as they disappeared behind the frothy waterfall. I imagined tomorrow's headline about a stupid Chicago widow and her three drowned boys. But just when I was about to run to the guide for help, the kids emerged sputtering, cursing, and still clinging to the log.

At dinner, the seven-year-old slathered ketchup on the buffalo burger he'd ordered on a dare. One of the boys farted loudly and everyone in the restaurant glared at us. We laughed as if we were back in our own airtight house, at our own Shaker table, back before the stroke. I thanked God the boys so bravely faced life's dangers: a mule ride down a canyon wall, rafting on a hollow log in ancient water, the death of their father.

Before we headed back to the cabin, we gathered on the canyon overlook. The boys fell as silent as startled deer. The sun had already set, and the perfect darkness was both fearsome and familiar. Above us, the stars shimmered from the graveyard of space. The charcoal abyss below sucked away all sound. My blood rivered in the deep crevice of the ancient stone. Feeling the pull of eternity, I reached for the anchor of my children.

The blackness above was forever; the blackness below was home.

THE DISAPPEARING GIRL

MY MINIVAN CHURNS IMPATIENTLY AS I WAIT IN THE long queue. Up ahead, it's easy to spot my daughter in the gaggle of starched, school-crested shirts and navy-blue pants. She's the only one with brown eyes and skin to match. She's the only one whose thick, black hair is tamed into stiff braids.

She is standing apart, her eyes scanning the row of cars, a refugee on a hostile shore waiting for an airlift. When she finally sees our car, she shoulders her heavy book bag—too full of academic pressure for a fourth grader—and a smile lands on her face. She is not ashamed to show me the beautiful Wolof gap in her front teeth. She waves desperately, as if otherwise I might miss her, the lone black child in a sea of white.

Finally, she opens the door and jumps into the back seat. "How was your day?" I say brightly, swallowing the stress of having to pick her up from private school every afternoon. She buckles in and opens her daily treat—today it's a bag of Doritos and bottled tea. No time to get to the store for apples. Bad mom.

She says nothing, but munches quietly and looks out the window. We pass the blond girls yelling things out of car windows like "Call me if you want to go riding!" or "Don't forget your swimsuit!"

At ten, my daughter wants, more than anything, to be chosen. She has a crush on Henry Frank (the kids call him HankFrank, as if it were one word). My daughter has a chance with HankFrank because he is funny-goofy, already eccentric, probably gay.

I turn off the radio, which I always do when the kids are in the car, just in case something bubbles up from their mysterious lives. Lately, my daughter has become impenetrable. When I hug her, she stiffens. Even though I am her lifeboat, she will not touch me. She is the kind of lonely that cannot be explained, so it becomes someone else's fault. Mine.

"Did you know that I am invisible?" Her words come in a scratchy little-girl voice, but she is too old for make-believe. She is stating a fact. My heart is a block of ice. I glance at her in the rearview mirror. She keeps eating Doritos vacantly.

Suddenly, I am six. It is 1967 and my first-grade teacher, Mrs. Houston, is so severe, every inch of me wants to please her.

I figure out after the first day that I am smarter than the other kids. The white kids. Every day, I want to prove my worth to Mrs. Houston by giving her the right answers. She calls on the other children; I don't understand why she doesn't see me. I stretch my hand higher, accent my eagerness with a few "Ooh, oohs," but still she gazes over my head to the dolt behind me with the ruby curls.

This is not what I had imagined when I'd longed to go to school. I'd dreamed of friends and books and scissors and the sweet smell of paste. I dreamed of chalk scraping on the board and gold stars on my homework. I never dreamed I would disappear.

My daughter finishes her Doritos and crumples the bag loudly. I stop the car in front of the manicured lawn of a stranger. I get out and open my daughter's door. She tracks me wide-eyed, afraid that she is in trouble. I unlock her seat belt and pull her out of the car. Her classmates peer at us curiously as they drive by in their moms' SUVs. She doesn't know it yet, but after today, my daughter will never see them again.

I take her shoulders and gaze into her eyes. I look at her so long that the hard resentment of her spine bends toward me. Her anger softens to tears.

"I can see you," I say, taking her into my arms.

GRAVEYARD LOVE

JAN SMILED UP AT STEVE AS HE GENTLY PLACED A CUP of tea on the end table. The waft of bergamot encircled her as he kissed her forehead.

"Your Earl Grey, my queen!" he said, nodding respectfully.

"Thanks, honey," she said, sighing deeply as she reached for the bone-china cup and saucer.

Steve poked at a log in the fireplace, then picked up his newspaper, groaning slightly as he settled back into his easy chair. Jan sipped her tea and closed her eyes as the warmth slid toward her heart. Pulling her angora shawl close, she returned to her historical novel.

This is what their Saturday evenings were like now that the girls were nearly gone. The flurry of invitations to dinner parties and charity galas had waned as each daughter graduated, and the pull of social obligations became no contest for the gentle gravity of their fireplace.

It was a good time in their lives, but sometimes Jan was afraid to count her blessings. Elise had been their worst, with her tinderbox of red hair, her volatile worldview, her scruffy boyfriends from the nearby public school. And Kara, good heavens! Secret tattoos, a nose piercing, and clothes that were somehow kind to people in the

Third World. But both girls managed to graduate from Brookside Prep without public incident. Varsity field hockey, AP classes, and the homecoming court, as expected. They'd escaped parenthood relatively unscathed, if you didn't count Elise's DUI, which Steve had been able to get dismissed by a probate judge. Or Kara's trip to the gynecologist for that nasty little infection.

At the hum of the garage door, Steve put down his paper and glanced at his watch. "She's back already?"

"Hey, Mom! Hey, Dad!" Their youngest, Taylor, clamored into the den, bringing in a whoosh of cool autumn air with her. Jan couldn't help but feel a little disappointed. She'd had the urge to cuddle with Steve, but now . . .

"Hello, Mr. and Mrs. Kent." Leesa followed closely behind Taylor. The two had been at the Montessori together, and then at Prep, both the lower and upper school. But it was only in their junior year that they'd become joined at the hip. "It seems we're never going to run out of daughters," Steve had said after Leesa became a fixture in their house.

"Hi, girls," Jan said, dog-earing a page in her book. "Back so soon?"

They smiled at each other coyly. "The party was boring," Taylor said. "We decided on scary movies and popcorn."

Jan had always thought they were a strange pair. Taylor had the lean, athletic build of a distance runner. A typical youngest child, she had a tendency to rail at the rules and push the limits. Taylor was pretty in a chiseled way, but she wore no makeup, and even now, her hair was tussled like she'd just spent the night in the back seat of a car.

Leesa was more level-headed, less complicated. Not really pretty, but so endearing that her wide mouth and saucer eyes could be forgiven. Jan and Steve agreed: Leesa was a good influence on Taylor, a nice girl who colored within the lines.

"C'mon, Leese," said Taylor, dragging her girlfriend upstairs. Then, calling back at her parents, she added, "She's spending the night!"

"Those two," said Steve, going back to his paper.

Jan tried to concentrate on her book, but all she could do was listen to the girls giggling upstairs. It was funny how relaxed she and Steve were when it came to raising Taylor. As the eldest, Elise had borne the full brunt of their neuroticism as parents: the fear that one drunken night would rob their daughter of a diploma; that a misguided, graveyard love would saddle her with a bad husband and a swollen belly. That's why as soon as they were fifteen, Jan had trotted all of her girls to Dr. Henderson for birth control.

But even with her free spirit and willfulness, Taylor never pushed those buttons for Jan. Of all the girls, Taylor seemed less interested in dates and more focused on adventure. As long as Taylor held on to her best friend, Leesa, Jan had a sense that everything would be OK.

Suddenly, there was a loud thump overhead—like a football tackle or someone falling out of the bed—followed by uproarious laughter.

"What in the world are they doing up there?" Steve took off his glasses and frowned at the ceiling.

Jan laughed and turned the page of her novel. *They're staying out of trouble*, she thought.

NOCTURNE

AT AGE SEVEN, JEANINE LOST THE FAMILY DOG. SHE HAD been practicing scales on the piano—eyes closed and head bent toward the music—when her mother yelled from the kitchen that it was time to walk Smoky. The spell broken, Jeanine pushed away from the piano, gave her parka a furious zip, then yanked the purple leash from its hook. Smoky, who was ink and ivory just like the keys of her Yamaha, danced urgently. Once outside, Jeanine smacked Smoky with the leash instead of hooking it to his collar. "Stupid dog," she pouted. Smoky cocked his leg to the snow, then nipped happily at the leash. They hadn't gone a block before Smoky pointed, then dashed after a sleek squirrel. Jeanine ran after him until her heart was on fire and her toes burned with cold. She wailed his name, but Smoky kept running.

Jeanine was thirteen when she lost the citywide Chopin competition to Grace Lee. Grace played the dreamlike Nocturne in D Flat Major, a piece that Jeanine had considered before opting instead for the Etude in F Major, which made her heart sing. Grace, whose performance was mechanical but flawless, got to compete at the New York Grand Prix for a chance to play at Carnegie Hall. Jeanine got a second-place trophy to put on her piano. She tried not to cry as she and Grace posed for pictures for the *Evanston Gazette*. Everyone congratulated Jeanine for doing so well, but she couldn't forgive herself for putting passion ahead of perfection.

At age nineteen, Jeanine lost her virginity to a pimple-pocked math major from Scranton. A sophomore at Northwestern, she hadn't wanted to look like a novice when the real moment arrived, hopefully with Brandon Kyles, the organ major who always lingered outside of her practice room. It turned out that the boy from Scranton had been a virgin, too—something Jeanine hadn't counted on. Their fumbling tryst was as chaffing as a pelvic exam. Afterward, she pushed the gangly, shuddering young man away and never spoke to him again.

Jeanine was twenty-seven when she miscarried her first child, twenty-nine when she lost her second. At night, she spooned with her husband, Brandon, and feared that she was being punished for not wanting children enough. "It's OK," Brandon whispered into the darkness. "It just means you have more time for your music." For years, a dream shook her awake every morning: two faceless children running in the snow, dragging an empty leash behind them.

It was a good thing Jeanine lost her keys. If she hadn't, she would have been on time to pick up the twins from camp. And then she would have been among the mothers who first got the news of the eight-car pileup on I-94. She would have spent an interminable forty minutes at the school parking lot wondering if Leila and Lucas were bloodied in a ditch beside the freeway—or worse. Eventually, she'd found her keys, which were on the floor by the piano, beneath leaves of music. She sped to meet the kids, feeling guilty that she had spent their week at camp thinking about performing again. When Jeanine arrived, the bus was just rolling in. The mothers with red, swollen eyes clapped their prayerful hands and cheered. The twins were hanging from the window and calling out her name.

When the woman at the jewelry counter asked her if she was sure she wanted to reset her marquis-diamond engagement ring, Jeanine nearly lost it. What? Did the woman think that maybe the divorce would be undone, that the ring would once again slide easily over the knuckle of trust? "I'm sure," Jeanine said tersely. "Just do it."

Most of the time, Jeanine felt lucky that she had only lost one breast and a head full of hair. Not even Leila's terrified tears, or the dim silences that spaced Lucas's long-distance calls made her feel sad. But some mornings, when the snow laced the windowpanes and the aching went deeper than her bones, she listened to Chopin and ran her hand against the hollow of her chest, wishing, wishing that she'd had more time to practice.

POSTBELLUM LOVE STORY

PEEKING THROUGH THE STAINED-GLASS PORTAL OF their Chesterfield home, Toya watched the unmarked squad car drop off her husband under the cover of darkness. Affably, Clarence unfolded himself from the back seat and Toya noticed how, even now, he took the time to shake the hand of the burly cop. Always a politician.

As Clarence wobbled toward her, Toya realized that her love for him had long fermented to pity. There would be a headline the next morning about how Clarence Hardwick—a shoo-in to become the state's first black US senator—had picked up another DUI. It was a mark of how far some African Americans had come, that the suburban police officer hadn't hauled him straight to jail.

She stood in the doorway as he approached. Already, he was glazed with the hunger for another drink. She could let him in or kick him out. This was it—her moment to escape.

When Toya was fourteen, she had been sitting in eighth-grade history class when Heather, the freckly captain of the County Day field-hockey team, asked why Africans had bought and sold each other into slavery. Other questions percolated: Why didn't the slaves just commandeer a ship and go back home? And if things were so bad in the South, why didn't they all just run away?

"I definitely woulda run," said Philip, whose authority was cemented by the light tinge of a mustache. The others chimed in, agreeing, but the chorus was missing one voice.

Toya's.

Why would anyone endure being enslaved? she wondered. Of course, the answer was *love*. Slavery times were not like these, when mothers could run away from home to find themselves but still Skype once a week and send birthday cards and Christmas gifts. In the time of slavery, escape meant you had to leave behind everyone that you loved and probably never see them again.

Toya doubted that Heather, with her slap shot, or Phil, with his almost-mustache, would have gone anywhere if it meant being alone. But as the only African American in the class, she didn't want to be pegged as hostile—like the bossy black women on reality shows. That would mean no more invitations to parties, or chatty sleepovers, or weekends at the mall.

So when everyone looked to Toya for her opinion, she just shrugged and said nothing.

At the front door, Toya waited for Clarence to say something —anything.

But he only stood there swaying slightly with his head down and tears raining, a refugee on his own doorstep. A neighbor's car turned into the cul-de-sac, and Toya quickly pulled him inside.

In that moment, she realized that her mother had done the easy thing by leaving. Toya was much stronger. Long past the day when she had stopped loving Clarence, she'd found other loves to bind her. Love of their happy children, with their riding lessons and camping trips. Love of their sprawling home, so tastefully appointed. Love of her heirloom tomatoes and bright holiday parties. Love of being a revered black family in this sea of white incredulity.

She touched Clarence gently on the shoulder, and he nodded gratefully before stumbling upstairs to the bedroom. She watched him shakily ascend, knowing that in order to keep everything she loved, she would need to be there for Clarence tomorrow, and all the tomorrows after.

Just as she'd suspected in middle school—she was no runner.

The history teacher had finally made the class settle down by telling them the story of Harriet Tubman. How the woman they called "Moses" ran away from the Maryland plantation rather than risk being sold. Harriet worked in Philadelphia, saved her money, and went back to rescue her sister and her sister's children. On a second trip, she ushered her brother and two other men to freedom. On her third trip, she went back for her husband.

Fourteen-year-old Toya had never heard this version of the story, and her heart startled. Even Harriet Tubman had realized that freedom wasn't worth the price of abandoning her family, so she'd come back home. She'd risked it all for love.

But when Harriet stole back to her old plantation, she discovered her husband with another woman. He refused to come with her.

As Toya listened to the story, she broke down. Her classmates thought she was crying about the slaves, but she wasn't.

SECOND
SLEEP

YOU WAKE TO DARKNESS. THE MOON TINGES YOUR room cadaver blue, but beneath your closed door seeps the warm amber of a hearth. People are talking.

You sit up. Yes, it is the smell of tender roasts, spicy pies. Laughter reeks. The ghosts have arrived without an invitation. There is too much night to let it go to waste.

You put your bare feet on the floor, not wanting to risk a sound— not even the shuffle of slippered feet. You shiver, but the cold is coming from your bones and cannot be shaken.

Downstairs you creep, and from the landing, the party is brightly offending.

Mama is aproned, her hair caught up in a scarf. Brother Man eats from everyone's plate but his own. He is gaunt, the way you last saw him—but without the bullet hole. Maybe that's why he is full of smiles. Missy's cheeks are pink from being pinched. She is passed from lap to lap, like a warm potato.

You had been afraid that your presence would poison the gathering, but the spirits don't seem to notice your waft of sorrow and lavender. There is an empty seat at the table that has always been yours. You slide into it. Midyarn, Aunt Sister passes you a hunk of skillet cornbread.

It's been years since you relaxed in the breast of family, but the dark cloak of December helps you remember. There was once something called a holiday, and the jokes about your cooking were the thing of family lore. The taunting used to make you blaze like a fresh wick. But on this night, you can hear the sweetness in the jesting. Like a pinch of sugar in the bitter greens.

From behind you, two arms slide around your waist. There is a humid breath on your neck, wide palms cup your breasts. Now in your bones, a fire. You lean back against the hard chest. He has come home.

The party disappears. In the old shotgun house, people always knew how to be scarce. He brings you down with a whisper. His kiss is as deep as forever. He plunges you into yesterday, and then, with the brittle snow, he is gone.

The moon has spoken her mind. There is nowhere to go but back into night.

TO THE
BONE

DAILY, A PIECE OF CRACKLING BREAD, A BOWL OF BOILED turnips, fried fatback. Pa and the boys would get extra pieces of the salty meat whenever there was any to be had. They worked at the mill and needed their strength. Sometimes Pa would save the tough meat rinds and sneak them to me before he left for work. Whenever I'd feel faint while boiling shirts, I'd stick a piece in my mouth, letting the smoky flavor of his kindness fill me up. I learned early how to live on bone and gristle.

At least I got to suck the marrow of bones and gnaw on juicy gristle. Aletha Ruffin was so skinny, her cheeks sunk in where her teeth used to be. They called her Chicken Legs. Her hair was a thin nest of wire and husk. When she smiled, you thought death was coming. Once, Mama sent me to school with a buttermilk biscuit stuffed with pear preserves, and Aletha let the waters of her mouth run, just like a dog waiting for scraps at the back door. What could I do but give it to her? She grabbed the biscuit without a thank you and never looked me in the eye again. They say the county came and took away the Ruffin children, but sometimes I wonder if they just dwindled down to nothing and disappeared.

There are ways to keep from dwindling down to nothing. Eat from the root, savor the skins. Feast on gizzards, tongues, and hearts. Sop your bread in pot liquor. Scrape crackling from the pan to make gravy taste like a meal. Lard your belly. Trade a dime for a pickle so sour it will lock your jaws. When your eyes start to sparkle and your hips round out, sway sweetly in front of a man, like a ripened berry ready to be plucked.

The blackberries were ripe for plucking the summer I swayed in front of Thalius Jones. In the back of his uncle's pickup, he sunk his teeth into my tender flesh and gripped the rounds of my hips. "Girl, you give a man something to hold on to," he said. That Christmas, he brought Mama two bright oranges, and Pa a bunch of raisins still on the vine. We got married in the spring. When I sat at the table with Thalius, he spooned his turnips into my bowl. "Eat up," he said. "I'ma have me a big, fat baby."

Tessie was a big, fat baby. Everywhere I went, folks would draw in a breath and say, "Ooh-wee. Look at that girl!" I'd shine her up with Vaseline, gather her thick hair in a bow, and parade her at the five-and-dime. I walked one-sided with her on my hip. When Thalius would come home in the evenings from the post office, the kitchen would be heavy with the smell of fried pork chops and onions. He'd holler, "Where's my big-boned girls?" Until the day she grew up and got married, Tessie would always run to him first. He'd take her moon face with both hands, let his thumbs run over her velvet skin, and tell her that she was the prettiest girl in the world.

My granddaughter, Madison, has the velvety complexion that her mom always had, and a face as wide and self-satisfied as the moon's. She used to let me pinch her delicious thighs, and she blushed when Thalius called her "Pork Pie." But now Madison's thirteen and growing up; she gets mad at the things that used to make her smile. Last week, I took her school shopping for a pair of those jeans that fit like the skin of an onion. The lady in the store frowned and said, "We don't carry those in large sizes, sweetie." The moon went into shadow, and I couldn't cheer Madison up even with a bowl of Häagen-Dazs.

The moon is shadowed by evening clouds as I set a bowl of my home cooking in front of Madison. At sixteen, she is now so thin, I worry how she will ever become a blackberry, ripe for picking. "Eat," I say, spooning Madison more food. She eyes my prosperous waist. "No thanks, Nanny," she says politely. Her eyes have no sparkle, like the eyes of the alabaster girls in magazines. She pushes around the food I have cooked for her, but I eat without shame: braised turnips, ham, and crackling bread.

REQUIEM FOR A DRESS

WHAT IS TODAY—TUESDAY? I GUESS I'D BETTER GET UP and do the laundry if I'm going to be ready when Margie comes to take me to see Zoe. Margie is such a stickler for time. Maybe it's because she's my oldest.

Now, she's nothing like my Zoe. I remember the day Zoe was born—I'd never seen such a grove of fine red hair on such a tiny, pale scalp. Like shoots of bleeding heart blooming in white sand. I can't wait to see her today. I never get to see the girls now that they have families of their own.

Who moved my purse again? Is today Monday? When Margie gets here, I'm going to ask her to stop coming to my house and moving my things. Last week, I think she left the stove on. Nearly burned the dickens out of my palm when I touched the hot eye. Margie thinks she always has to check on me, but I don't need her butting in, turning my life upside down.

I like this dress with the bright yellow daisies, or are those black-eyed Susans? Didn't Zoe have on a dress just like this for her graduation party umpteen years ago? I'll have to remember to ask her when I see her today. Somewhere I think I have a picture of her in it. She was so slender and beautiful, her hair like auburn fire. She's my favorite, although a mother isn't supposed to say so. Margie is the stickler, but Zoe is the . . .

Where's the dog? *Lady? Lady!* Don't tell me that she got out again. Margie's going to be mad at me. I swear, that dog is going to give me a heart attack one day. *Lady?* Not under there . . . I'll never forget that Christmas that Larry came home dressed like Santa with that fat puppy under his arms. Lord, Zoe couldn't stop squealing! To have a plump, honey-haired retriever delivered to her by Santa on Christmas Eve. That was the best Christmas ever. The best ever.

Whose dress is this? I'd better wash it before they come back for it. I won't add bleach, no sir. Don't want to wash out those loud daisies. Or are they black-eyed Susans?

Lady? She's been by my side ever since the night my dear Larry passed away. All that day, Lady just carried on, pacing and whimpering. We didn't know how to settle her down. Tried Milk-Bones, even a good smack with a rolled-up newspaper. Finally, I made Larry take her for another walk. That's the last time I saw my darling husband alive. An hour later, Lady came home alone, scratching at the door like the devil was after her. Soon as I heard her, I knew Larry was gone.

This dress is so busy. Who would buy a dress like this? Those flowers make it look so cheap. I'm going to have to ask Margie to give it to Goodwill. Where is she, anyway? Isn't it Thursday? She's late again.

Oh. Oh. My back. Let me sit down a minute. Just . . . God, I'm so alone. Larry's gone. The girls have moved away, and then I had to put Lady down. Her hip was as bad as mine is now. I miss that dog.

Maybe I'll just read the paper a minute. Nothing but bad news . . . crime and crooked politicians, that's all. And the obituaries—so sad. Look at this pretty woman, only forty years old, in her prime. Have you ever seen such lovely eyes and warm red hair? "Is survived

112

by her mother and sister." Her funeral is this afternoon. I'll bet her mother is beside herself. Lord help her.

No, I can't sit here. If I sit, I'll sink into sadness. Idle mind is the devil's workshop. Let me get up and get dressed. Margie told me to be ready by ten. Or maybe it was noon. She laid out this horrible black dress for me to put on, but who wants to go out looking all dowdy? I think I'll wear my favorite dress to surprise Zoe. The one with the daisies.

OPEN
SKY

BETTY PRESSED HER KNEES TOGETHER AS HER GRAND-daughter, Alex, knelt to pry off her shoes.

"C'mon, Gran," Alex coaxed patiently. "Lift your leg so I can slide off your shoe."

"Why do I have to take off my shoes to get on a plane?" Betty complained, her left bunion now exposed to the flying public.

"You might have a bomb in your Naturalizers," Alex said, grasping the other foot. "One more, Gran."

Betty lifted her right foot while her granddaughter removed the other shoe. The faint smell of pickles and Dr. Scholl's foot powder wafted upward. "This is the last time I'm flying anywhere, so help me," Betty mumbled.

The removal of her shoes, much to Betty's horror, was just the first indignity of air travel. Alex stripped Betty of her light summer sweater, her chiffon scarf, and her tapestry purse. Then Betty stepped into a glorified phone booth, set her legs an unladylike two feet apart, and raised her arms to display her short range of motion. It hurt.

"You're fine," a gruff TSA agent said, pointing to the other end of the conveyor belt. Betty waddled there, the soles of her stockinged feet arching uncomfortably away from the cold, filthy floor. She waited for Alex as their belongings clogged the conveyor.

"Whew, that's a job!" Alex breathed, giving her grandmother a smile. "C'mon, Gran, sit down over there while I get our stuff."

A young, athletic woman plopped down next to Betty and started lacing her tennis shoes. "That your granddaughter?"

"Yes, indeed," Betty gloated. "I'm taking her to Atlanta so that she can go to college."

"Wow, that's nice," the woman said. "I *love* Atlanta. How long are you staying?"

Betty was about to answer, but it suddenly occurred to her that she had no idea. She tried to remember, but it seemed the plans had come together so quickly. There had been the tumble in the bathroom in her Pittsburgh row house—a cracked fibula. Then rehab, then as soon as she could travel, the family in Georgia had talked her into accompanying Alex down South.

"Gran hasn't decided how long she's staying yet," said Alex, who suddenly appeared with their carry-ons. She planted a kiss on Betty's forehead.

Betty was warmed by her granddaughter's affection, but confused. She couldn't stay in Atlanta forever! She needed to get back to her missionary group at Greater Mt. Moriah AME. And the children at the community garden expected her to be there on Thursdays through the fall.

"Ready, Gran?" Alex led the way through the airport, measuring her steps to match her grandmother's. Betty remembered when it used to be the other way around. When she would have to climb the stairs slowly, then wait for Alex to scramble up on her plump legs. Now it seemed that Alex was always running ahead of everybody.

"Gran? Are you OK? You want me to call a skycap?"

"I'm fine, honey," Betty said, even though she wished they could stop and rest for a minute.

Once on board, Betty took the window seat. Alex buckled them in, then turned on her iPod. As the plane took off, Betty watched the world tilt. Her stomach roiled on a new axis, and she began to jitter with something that felt like excitement. She was going somewhere.

Soon the attendants began the cabin service. Betty was mesmerized by the women in their neat uniforms, their tightly wound hair and molten-red lips. To this day, she envied her classmate Sandy Jenkins, who had joined the air force and become a WAF in 1950. Betty had done the decent thing—gotten married right out of high school and stayed put. Thirty years with the Pittsburgh public schools with time off in the summer to raise the children, while Sandy missed the chance to settle down. Men questioned Sandy's virtue when they found out she'd spent five years in the air force. What a price to pay for seeing the world!

"What can I get you?" An attendant bent over their row. Betty stared at the woman's brilliant sapphire cocktail ring and French tips. Maybe if she had it to do over, Betty would put off marriage for a few years to become a flight attendant. She imagined herself strutting authoritatively up and down the narrow aisle calming babies, offering men used newspapers, and serving cold drinks—even wine!

"Gran, do you want a Sprite?" Alex asked, pulling out her earbuds. "And I'll have a Coke."

As soon as the flight attendant left, Betty elbowed Alex. "What do you suppose she studied in college to get a job like this?" she whispered discreetly. "Maybe you could study it, too. You could be like her one day."

Alex stared at Betty, then suddenly burst out laughing. "Are you serious, Gran? I'm going to film school. I'm not gonna be a *flight attendant!*"

Betty turned quickly to the window to hide the sting of her granddaughter's ridicule. For the rest of the flight, she peered silently at the sugar-white clouds and the endless open sky.

THE
MASSAGE

EMMA LAY STIFFLY ON HER BACK AND PULLED THE THIN sheet to her chin like a child afraid of monsters beneath the bed. The sheet sloped uphill from her saddlebag breasts to the apex of her stomach. She sucked in deeply, wishing that she had followed her right mind and joined the "Jammin' Ladies" at the rec center to shed a few pounds. But no, she had decided instead to sit and do scrapbooking all day. So here she was at the spa, a whale beached on a narrow table.

Her toes were cold. *You'd think they'd give you socks instead of wasting money on bottled water,* Emma thought. She closed her eyes and tried to quiet her mind, like Oprah recommended. But her thoughts drifted from puffy, white clouds to dinner. It was Friday—Harold would want fish tonight. What could she fix to go with it? Not slaw or even hush puppies now that she had to watch Harold's sugar. Maybe a salad with tomatoes from the garden, which she should be weeding right now, instead of wasting time and money on a silly massage.

Relax, she told herself. After all, this was supposed to be a gift, a spa day from the kids. "Spa," a useless word like orzo or pashmina. Emma thought of her mother, a laundress who'd raised three kids alone during the Depression. The only massage she'd ever gotten was when little Emma would rub her feet at night.

Emma's nose itched, but she didn't want to scratch it and risk someone seeing the skin flapping from the scaffolding of her upper arms. The room smelled of something spicy, vaguely herbal, and possibly illegal. Music painted the dimly lit room. Not exactly music, but the sound of oceans, stars, and morning birds. It made her think of dying.

"Good afternoon, Mrs. Anderson!" Startled, Emma clenched the muscles against her weak bladder. "Ready for your aromatherapy massage?"

The massage therapist was a girl-woman whose badge said, "Maya." Maya was reading the three-by-five card Emma had filled out when they traded her belongings for a locker key and a crest-emblazoned robe. "So this is your first massage? I see that your problem spot is your lower back. Just relax, you're going to love this," Maya said, discreetly folding back the sheet to expose the broad flatness of Emma's dark thigh. "Let me know if you're uncomfortable."

Maya was some version of white—Italian or maybe Arab? Emma recoiled at the thought of a white woman being so intimate with her; there was something unnatural about it. But as Maya eased her hands over Emma's leg, the touch was easy and familiar. Not like Harold's touch—his fingers were about as nimble as a roll of pennies. This was slow and gentle, each press a silent questioning: "Does it hurt here? Does this feel better?"

After about a half hour, Maya lifted the sheet to form a scrim. "Now turn over," she said. Emma forced her buttery muscles to move. She lodged her face down into the doughnut hole. Her palms faced upward and her toes pointed, like a mermaid gliding in emerald water.

When Maya pushed deep into the small of Emma's back, the older woman felt a quiver. It was as if she had always wanted someone to touch that place, that tight muscle where life's weight coiled.

The massage therapist's hands moved firmly up Emma's back and down again, loosening something primordial. Tears gathered in Emma's eyes, stinging her nose with their salty suddenness. This, then, was what it was like to be touched without desire or demand.

The room suddenly smelled of rose water, the way her mother used to smell on Sundays. "Ma'Dear?" Emma whispered. "Is that you?"

"What's that, Mrs. Anderson? I told you it would be wonderful!" Maya said. "Well, your time is up, but don't get up too fast. Take your time. Your robe is behind the door. Thank you and come again!"

There was the quiet click, then nothing but ocean, birds, and stars. Emma turned onto her side and curled into her nakedness as if she were waiting to be born.

ACKNOWLEDGMENTS

THE ART OF LIVING AND THE ART OF WRITING ARE SO often at odds, especially for women. I could never have pursued both without the love of my parents, the support of my brother, and the blessing of my children. Toni, here I am, just as you predicted. My soul mates in Writer's Bloc (Kelly Fordon, thanks for your special support!) gave me so much inspiration, while my Full Moon Sisters took care of my muse for twenty-five years. I have to thank Toi Derricotte and Cornelius Eady for welcoming me into the Cave Canem family, an experience that changed my life. Vievee Francis, you are a brilliant teacher and patient midwife. David Haynes, thank you for Kimbilio Fiction, where this book began to take shape.

I am profoundly grateful for the professional and personal support I have gained as a 2015 Kresge Artist Fellow, which was awarded by Kresge Arts in Detroit, a program of The Kresge Foundation.

M. L. Liebler, you are the literary godfather to so many, and I still don't understand how I came to be counted in that number. I am full of gratitude. And finally, Annie Martin, I treasure the faith you placed in this project from the start.

To all the women whose stories are never told, I honor your sacrifice with my words.